Suzanne had been daydreaming. . . .

Her eyes moved from his bobbing Adam's apple to his flushed face. He had obviously said something very important, but she had no idea what it had been.

"So. . .how do you feel about that, Miss Waters?" He was such a gentleman, always addressing her formally.

"Well. . . ," she hesitated, wondering how to react so he wouldn't know she hadn't been listening.

"I guess I'm speaking prematurely," he rushed on. "I know you have to see to your father, but, like I said, next year when I turn twenty-one, I'd like to ask for your hand."

She gulped, wondering how she could have possibly missed his proposal. She mentally scurried to recapture her wits, knowing the importance of choosing precisely the right words.

"Art—and please call me Suzanne from now on—you understand how worried I am now, with Pa and all."

"Oh, yes! I hope you don't think I'm being improper."

"No, not at all! I appreciate everything you've said, and I'm honored that you—" she broke off, swallowing. "I just think we should wait a while longer to discuss this. But, thank you." She gave him her best smile.

He was staring into her gray eyes, transfixed, blithely unaware that his size-twelve feet blocked the passage of the drunken cowboy stumbling past.

Suddenly, a crash just behind her jolted Suzanne, and she whirled to see a huge man sprawled across the adjoining table. A goblet shattered against a china plate; silver clattered to the floor.

PEGGY DARTY is the popular, award-winning author of nine novels and numerous magazine articles who also has extensive background in television and film. Darty, who makes her home in Alabama, debuts in **Heartsong Presents** with an historical titled *Morning Mountain*.

Morning Mountain

Peggy Darty

Heartsong Presents

A note from the Author:

I love to hear from my readers! You may write to me at
the following address: **Peggy Darty**
                            Author Relations
                            P.O. Box 719
                            Uhrichsville, OH 44683

ISBN 1-55748-768-5

MORNING MOUNTAIN

Cover illustration by Brian Bowman.

PRINTED IN THE U.S.A.

one

Suzanne Waters withdrew her leather glove and swiped her bleeding thumb across her jeans. She hated barbed wire, even if Pa and other Colorado ranchers declared it to be the greatest invention of the 1870s. She sighed, checking her handiwork. Through dogged persistence, she had managed to twist a sagging strand of wire back in place, and now Pa would never know how close they had come to losing their horses.

Ever since her father's accident, she had been riding over the range, checking to be sure there were no breaks in the fence or other calamities to add to their list of disasters. With their only ranch hand gone and Pa laid up with cracked ribs and a sprained ankle, she was praying long and hard.

A strand of blond hair had escaped her felt hat, tickling her sunburned forehead as it dangled over worried gray eyes. If not for a promise to her mother to "remain a lady," when Abigail Waters lay dying the past winter, she would grab the scissors and whack the long strands into a more practical style. A boys' cut, perhaps. After all, she was quickly falling into the role of the son her father wanted but never had.

Behind her, Nellie, her horse, nickered softly.

"We'll go soon," she promised, glancing over her shoulder to the beloved mare that had become her best friend in their new home. She had carried on some very serious conversations with patient Nellie, but Nellie, for once, was ignoring her.

"What's wrong?" Suzanne asked, noticing the way Nellie's ears were perked as the animal stared out across the valley.

Suzanne looked around, inspecting the landscape. At the base of Morning Mountain, the terrain spread into a valley, enclosed by walls of pine, cottonwood, and aspens. Beyond the woods lay the road to Wiley's Trading Post two miles down the road. Suzanne frowned. She could see a horse moving through the trees, toward the end of the woods. Soon the horse would reach the clearing and she'd be able to see the rider.

"Just someone headed to the post, Nellie." Suzanne stroked the mare's neck then turned her attention back to her sore thumb.

The bleeding had stopped and she pulled on her glove. As she wiggled her fingers into the warm leather, she glanced again toward the woods.

First the head, then the body of a black horse emerged. Suzanne frowned. There was something odd about the rider. She squinted, trying to determine what it was. Something about the rider bothered her. What? The rider sat on the horse, leaning forward like one afraid of falling—a rare sight in ranching country.

She pulled her hat brim lower on her forehead, shutting out the sun's rays for a better look.

The horse was in plain view now, and she realized the rider had slumped forward. Something was wrong with that rider.

Suzanne bit her lip, torn between Pa's warning to stay away from strangers and her own basic desire to help wherever she was needed. Glancing at the saddle scabbard that held her rifle, she felt safe enough to investigate. Gathering Nellie's trailing reins, she swung astride and kneed her mare.

Nellie, sensitive to her rider, stretched her legs until the two were a gray streak across the upper end of the valley. Suzanne was an excellent rider, spending hours on Nellie's back. Horse and rider knew each other well, and now Nellie sensed a crisis.

"Whoa," Suzanne called as they drew near the black stallion. By now, the man was barely hanging on. Even from a distance, she could see a trail of blood along the front of his shirt.

"What's happened?" she called, drawing rein. She jumped down and approached him cautiously.

The man was tall and well-built, dressed in a blue cotton shirt, dark pants, and leather boots. He wore a wide-brimmed, black hat, shading the face that slumped onto his chest.

She took a step closer. Dark hair tumbled over his forehead. His eyes were closed. Beneath a mustache, his mouth was partially open, as if asleep. But this man wasn't just asleep. He had lapsed into unconsciousness, unable to respond to her. She could see the mass of blood, clotting his shirt to his chest.

His horse stopped walking and turned wary eyes to Suzanne.

She approached the horse, stroking the dark gray patch on his forehead. Then she looked up at the man. He was bleeding on the left side; his right hand had gone slack on the reins. Another minute and he'd be on the ground.

"Hold on," she called, reaching up to steady him. "Can you hear me?"

She stared bewildered at the dark hair and neatly trimmed mustache. He was a handsome man, probably in his middle to upper twenties, with high cheekbones, straight nose, and full lips beneath the mustache.

"Mister, I'm taking you to the ranch," she said, wondering if he would be alive by the time she got him there.

ð

Hank Waters thrust his handmade crutch solidly onto the board floor and hobbled from the living room back to the bedroom. He paused in the doorway, studying the stranger who now occupied his bed. His daughter stood at the bedside, adjusting the bandages she and Hank had just wrapped around the man's left side.

"Suzanne, your ma couldn't have stood by and watched me dig that bullet out of him like you did." Hank's voice was gruff, as usual, but Suzanne heard the unmistakable note of pride.

"Guess I'm more like you than Mom," she answered distractedly, her attention focused on her patient.

The man had turned his head on the pillow, as though aware of their words. Suzanne watched him closely. His dark lashes parted slowly, and the bluest eyes she'd ever seen stared into her face. Everything about this man had been a surprise. He had the broadest shoulders she'd ever touched, for starters, and beneath the firm skin, his muscles were taut. She wondered what he did for a living; she wondered, even more, what had gotten him shot.

His dark brows drew together in confusion as he looked from Suzanne to her father, who was limping to the bed.

"Just lie still," she said, smiling at him. "Can you sip some water?"

A muffled sound drifted over his cracked lips, which she interpreted as a yes. She reached for the tin cup of water on the bedside table.

"Here, I'll hold his head," Hank offered, cradling the man's head in his brawny hands. Hank was tall and wiry, muscular and strong for a man of sixty years.

Suzanne pressed the brim of the cup to the stranger's lips.

"Sip it slowly," she warned, gently tilting the cup.

She watched with concern as the water trickled over his tongue, and he began to gulp.

"No!" She withdrew the cup. "You'll be sick if you drink too quickly."

Hank's sharp eyes, the same steel gray as his hair and beard, swept his daughter. "You oughta go back up to Denver and work in a hospital."

"Then who'd take care of you?" she shot back.

"I don't need—"

The stranger began to cough, interrupting their argument. Their bantering was comfortable and frequent, as native to the cabin as the smell of beeswax, and coffee brewing on the stove.

"What's your name, mister?" Hank barked as the man's head sank into the pillow, and his eyes closed.

Suzanne put a hand on her father's arm and shook her head.

"Let him sleep," she whispered.

"He's weak," Hank lowered his voice, "lost a lot of blood."

While Suzanne had restrained her father from asking questions, she found herself every bit as curious as Hank, perhaps even more. She checked the bandages—clean white strips of cloth improvised from an old sheet. The bleeding had stopped, thank God. She sighed with relief, pulling the quilt over his chest and motioning her father out of the room.

"Reckon I'll move my stuff out to the living room," Hank grumbled, hobbling to the pine wardrobe.

"Pa, I'll do that," Suzanne quickly offered. "You go lie down. At the moment, one patient is enough."

For once, Hank's stubborn streak refused to assert itself, allowing his daughter to take over. She stared after his thin frame, noticing how his shoulder blades jutted against his shirt. If not for a wide tight belt, his pants would never stay on. She wondered, worriedly, just how much weight he had lost since he'd begun working his daylight to dark regime, the labor backbreaking with no help.

God is our refuge and strength. The verse came to her mind; it was on the list she had made from her mother's Bible. Those verses had been all that had sustained her after her mother's death, and she found herself quoting them on a daily basis.

She followed her father out of the room, closing the door softly behind her. Hank had settled onto the front porch step and sat staring out at the valley, puffing on his pipe.

two

Luke Thomason tried to wedge his mind from the nightmare that had gripped him for. . .he had no idea how long. There had been a woman—or had she been an angel? A woman with beautiful blond hair and a kind smile. Had she given him something to drink?

His mind tumbled backward and again he was trapped in that nightmare, unable to escape.

A kerosene lamp hung over the poker table, casting a yellow glow on the cards in Luke's hand. He couldn't believe his luck. He had another winning hand. With a pair of jacks and two eights and another card coming, he could end up with a full house; or if not, he still had two pairs. He glanced at the card lying face down on the table. That card would tell the tale. Smoothly, he reached down, lifted it, and tucked the card among the others. *A jack!*

His mouth was dry, his palms were moist. He dared not move for fear of betraying his excitement. What was he doing here playing poker for high stakes when his experience had been limited to the bunkhouse at Godfrey's ranch?

Slowly, he lifted his eyes, studying the faces of the men at the table, trying to read their eyes. They had acquired the poker faces he'd heard about, but then he'd been told he had one too. With him, the inscrutable expression had been stamped on years before, by a determination to hide the ache from a heart that had been ripped in two.

The two men, directly to his left and right, wore range clothes. He sensed their lives were similar to his—dirt-poor ranch hands dreaming of wealth at the tables. The man opposite him was from Denver and a thoroughly unlikable sort.

Dressed in a black frock coat and white linen shirt, he was a small man, barely over five feet tall, with a superior attitude and an insulting manner. A nervous twitch pulled at the man's thin face, and put constant movement into the close-set black eyes. Those eyes jumped from player to player, back to his cards, then to the chips on the table. The eyes shot to his dwindling stack of chips then sank again to the cards in his hand.

The city slicker with the money was losing badly. And Luke, drawing from instincts and a sharp mind, was winning it.

The two men beside him were down to a handful of chips. Luke studied the twin stacks of chips piled high before him.

He counted out an impressive stack and placed them in the center of the table. Their faces didn't betray them, but he could feel the disappointment settling over the other players. He had just upped the price of poker, forcing a show of hands.

"I'm out," the man next to him said, coming to his feet. "I'm not losing the rest of my money."

The other ranch hand stood slowly, grabbing his one remaining chip and pocketing it quickly.

"Me, too."

The city slicker stayed in the game, adding a stack of chips to the pile in the center.

Smoothly, Luke laid out his full house, and the little man's eyes bulged. He began to cough, looking and sounding as though someone were choking him to death. His wrist went limp, dropping the cards onto the table. Luke was looking at two pairs. He had won again.

Luke was not a gambler by nature, and while the game was a challenge, he knew the danger as well. He was a poor, hardworking cowhand who had hit a streak of luck. But he knew when to quit.

He stood, gathering up his winnings. "Think I'll cash in," he said, glancing at the red-faced man across the table.

The little man leaped to his feet, sputtering with rage. "You can't quit now!"

Luke towered over him, his blue eyes narrowed. "Beg your pardon," he drawled, "but I can quit anytime I want to. . ."

A soft touch moved across his forehead, and the vague aroma of wild flowers filled his nostrils. Was he lying in a meadow? If so, who was touching him? That touch had soothed him, calmed him, freed him at last from the nightmare. He sank deeper into the pillow and found the peaceful sleep he craved.

three

Suzanne left the room again, closing the door softly behind her. Worriedly, she plodded out to the porch, where her father sat on the slab-log step, smoking his pipe.

"Pa, you've had experience with cowboys who took a bullet or got a bad injury riding bronc," Suzanne said, dropping down beside him. "Do you think an infection will set up in that man's shoulder?"

Hank squinted at her over a wisp of smoke. "Hard to tell. With all the alcohol we used, I'm guessing we've killed the germs."

"I rubbed down his horse then put him in the back corral so he and Rocky wouldn't tangle over the mares."

"Did you find a wallet on him or some identification?"

Suzanne shook her head. "Nope. There was a Colt revolver tucked in his bedroll and some personal items in his saddlebags, but nothing to tell us who he is."

"Wonder what happened?" Hank said, tapping the ashes from his pipe.

"I'm sure he'll tell us when he's able."

Hank frowned. "You say he had no money on him?"

Suzanne shook her head.

"He was robbed, then. Figured that when I saw he'd been shot in the back."

Suzanne lifted her eyes north to the sprawling mountain range of Pikes Peak. It was a wild and beautiful country, with its towering, snow-capped peaks and lush valleys of aspen and cottonwood. The problem was everyone wanted to settle in Colorado, and men were killing each other over homestead claims and water rights.

"Su-zanne," Hank said, drawing out her name the way he often did before making a point, "I'm saddling Rocky in the morning and getting back to work."

"Pa, you've got to give those cracked ribs time to heal. And your ankle is still too swollen for a day's punishment in the stirrups. I just hope you didn't do any damage to yourself when you helped me drag that man into the bedroom."

Hank turned and frowned at her. "Daughter, I'm getting tired of being bossed."

Suzanne jumped up from the step and began to pace the board porch. "Pa, I don't mean to be bossy, but you just won't take care of yourself. You should have known better than to try to break that mustang."

"Girl, I've broken more mustangs than you've counted years," he snapped. His gray eyes, faded by sun and wind, blazed with defiance. "When a mustang lopes into my valley, with us desperate for horses...I ain't letting him get away if I can stop him."

But you couldn't stop him, Suzanne thought, biting her lip. *Not anymore, Pa.*

While she had wisely refrained from speaking the words, Hank Waters, nevertheless, seemed to read her mind. He heaved a sigh and dropped his head to stare at his bandaged ankle.

"Well, Wilbur's got to live with his conscience and that can't be easy," he said at last. "But sometimes it's hard work keeping the anger out of my soul."

Suzanne reached over and placed a gentle kiss on her father's bearded cheek. "Uncle Wilbur will pay for what he did, Pa. Anger would just harm us, not him."

Hank's thin face softened with tenderness as he slowly turned to face his daughter. "You're so much like your ma. Just don't ever be as gullible."

Suzanne drew a deep breath. "Ma's love for her only brother blinded her to his faults."

Hank snorted. "And, like a fool, I took his word, sight unseen, that he had enough horses here to start a breeding ranch; and as for this cabin. . . ," his voice trailed as he sank into silence.

"We'll make it work, Pa," Suzanne spoke with conviction, drawing upon her optimistic nature. They *would* make it work, somehow. "We've survived the winter and Ma. . ." She swallowed hard and plunged on, "The worst is over."

Hank shook his head, but he looked unconvinced.

"Come on, Pa, cheer up. I'm making dumplings tonight. Life can't be all bad."

For the first time in days, a tiny smile touched Hank Waters' thin lips. "Dumplings? You trying to impress that young buck in there?"

The defiance on Hank's face minutes before was now mirrored in the expression of his only child. Hank saw it and smiled to himself, secretly pleased by his daughter's spirit.

"I don't try to impress any man," she stated, before turning on her heel and hurrying inside the cabin.

She headed across the L-shaped room which served as living room and kitchen and fought the frustration she felt. In truth, her father had struck a nerve. How she'd like to impress this handsome stranger, but it would be a waste of time to let her mind wander in such a direction. Her eyes drifted toward the closed door of the bedroom as she recalled the items in his saddlebags: a compass, a few toiletries, and a gold wedding band.

Upon seeing the ring, a keen disappointment had filled her. While it was ridiculous to have any romantic notions about a stranger—one who had been shot—she had been unable to stop herself from speculating. And then she'd found the ring. Oh well, a woman somewhere would thank them for saving his life. *Some lucky woman!*

four

Suzanne rolled over on the cot in her small bedroom and squinted at the daylight sifting through the muslin curtains above her bed. She reached up to part a curtain, curious about the weather. Gray clouds settled over Morning Mountain. She rubbed her eyes and tried to clear her mind, still fogged by sleep. Slowly, yesterday's strange events settled into her brain, and she bolted upright in bed, staring at the closed door of her bedroom. *The stranger!*

She swung her legs around and fumbled for her house shoes. The smell of coffee filled the cabin, a reminder of Hank's habit of rising early to drink a cup and watch the sunrise.

Suzanne reached into the wardrobe and removed a pair of clean pants and a cotton shirt. Her mother would roll over in her grave if she could see her dressed in the boys' clothes Suzanne had bought at the trading post. Still, there was no way she was going to muck out the stalls and ride over the range in a dress and petticoats. She shook her long blond hair back from her face, working the thickness into one fat braid at her nape. Her gray eyes ran over the clutter on her nightstand, wondering where the last grosgrain ribbon had landed. Abandoning the search, she grabbed a strip of leather and wound it around her braid.

She didn't care about clothes or being a lady right now; she had her father to think about. It was all she could do to keep him at home until he healed.

A muffled cough interrupted her thoughts. *The stranger!*

The front door closed, and she could hear Pa's crutch stamping over the board floors to the bedroom.

Suzanne crossed the living room and stood looking through the open door of the bedroom. Hank was seated in a chair by the bed, talking to the stranger who was propped up on the pillow, sipping coffee. His dark hair was swept back from his face, and his blue eyes looked alert, rested.

"You were lucky the bullet passed through your shoulder without striking a bone," Hank was saying.

As Suzanne paused in the door, the stranger's eyes lifted to her and he nodded politely.

"Mr. Thomason. . ." Hank began.

"Just Luke. . ."

"This is my daughter, Suzanne."

Suzanne smiled. "Hello."

He nodded. "Hello. Your father was telling me how you saved my life. I'm grateful."

"He's from Kansas," Hank said, twisting in his chair to survey his daughter. "On his way to Colorado Springs. Any low-down critter who'd shoot a man in the back..." Hank muttered, shaking his head.

Suzanne's eyes darted to the stranger, seeking his reaction. He had closed his eyes momentarily, as though trying to shut out some horrible memory. Then slowly he spoke.

"I should never have stopped in Bordertown."

"Bordertown?" Hank rasped. "No, son, you shouldn't have. That's an outlaws' hangout. You figure someone trailed you from there?"

Luke Thomason shook his head slowly as he stared across the room, obviously thinking back to two nights before. "The truth is, I got in a poker game. And I won. I rode out of town late at night. The guy I cleaned out must have followed me and waited till I made camp. I'd been in the saddle for two days; once I crawled in the bedroll, a herd of cattle could have stampeded behind me, and I wouldn't have heard."

"He shot you in your bedroll? But how did you. . . ?" Suzanne couldn't imagine someone would do such a thing. Maybe he didn't need to be talking about this. It had to have been a horrible experience.

"I hurt my back rodeoing this spring and—"

"Rodeoing?" Hank echoed, his gray eyes lighting up.

Suzanne studied her father's face, knowing he could barely contain his excitement. At last, he had someone under his roof who could talk rodeoing with him. These two could have a good time.

"Sleeping on the ground aggravated my back," the stranger continued, "so I put a pillow in my bedroll to support my shoulder."

"So the scoundrel sneaked up to shoot you in the back, not knowing about the pillow, and it slowed up the bullet," Hank finished, plowing a work-roughened hand through his gray hair.

"You think the man who shot you was the man from the poker table?" Suzanne asked.

Her mother would have said a lady did not pry, but she couldn't help it. After all, she'd invested quite a bit of time and effort in saving this man's life. She was curious to know just how he'd gotten himself into such a fix.

"I can't be sure," he answered. "I got shot, then I heard branches breaking and a horse taking off in the night. The man who lost his money to me looked like the kind who'd sneak up and shoot somebody in the back. And my wallet was the only thing missing." His eyes blazed with anger for a moment, then slowly the anger seemed to fade, replaced by an expression of. . .what? Suzanne wondered. Indifference? Yes, he looked indifferent to the conversation. It made her wonder how a person could slip from one emotion to another so quickly. Maybe he was the kind of man who tried to keep his thoughts private.

"He got your money?" Hank guessed.

"All of it." He stared into space for a moment then looked at Hank. "Exactly where am I?" he asked.

"Geographically speaking, you're at the foot of Morning Mountain," Hank said, absently rubbing his healing ribs. "We're about half a day from Bordertown. "Another day to Colorado Springs. But there's a trading post down the road that serves as stage stop, cafe, and general store. We can get a deputy out here. You'll be wanting to get a search on for the man who—"

"He's long gone by now," Luke sighed, staring into space.

Suzanne cleared her throat, trying to tactfully broach the subject. "Is there someone we should notify?"

He hesitated for a moment, studying his coffee cup. "No," he finally replied.

Suzanne was thinking of the gold wedding band. He had obviously decided not to alarm his wife now. "Then I'll get some breakfast," she said, heading for the door.

"Not for me," he called to her. "I'll be leaving as soon as. . ."

"Best not be thinking of getting on a horse just yet," Hank admonished. "You wouldn't make it far."

"Doc Browning stops by the post once a week, in case anyone in the area needs him," Suzanne said. "I'll leave word for him to come over."

"That won't be necessary," Luke replied. "You and your father have done a good job patching me up. I'll be all right."

Suzanne studied his pale face and doubted he felt as

healthy as he tried to appear. Her eyes moved to her father, who had fallen silent. Hank sat with his lips pursed, his eyes narrowed, looking at Luke Thomason.

"Pa, I'll get your breakfast," she said, turning from the room and walking back to the kitchen. Maybe the stranger wasn't hungry, but Hank would be wanting his biscuits and gravy, a ritual begun years ago by her mother and one he insisted on keeping.

five

Luke stared at the closed door, hating the abruptness in his voice, but he didn't know how to behave around these people. Nobody had ever done anything for him without expecting something in return. That's why he had told them, straight out, about the poker game and then getting shot and having his wallet stolen. He didn't like other people knowing his business, but he liked even less people expecting something from him when he couldn't oblige.

He sank deeper into the pillow, staring at the ceiling. They were decent people, or at least they seemed to be. Once they knew he couldn't repay them, maybe they'd quit being so nice. It was making him nervous.

He closed his eyes, remembering how soft her fingers had felt on his skin, remembering the smell of the sachet she wore. She smelled as sweet as honeysuckle, and he knew he'd better get out of here fast. He was still running from the Godfrey woman; he wasn't about to let someone else get ideas in their head about settling him down.

Of course this woman was different. . . .

He twisted nervously, and the pain in his left shoulder ripped through him. He sank his teeth into his lower lip, cursing his luck. He'd lost all his money, plus the winnings from the poker game, and now he'd gotten shot and was trapped in this bed for another day or two.

He opened his eyes and looked around the room. Something on the dresser caught his eyes. He scowled, growing even angrier.

Balancing the tray of food, Suzanne paused before the bedroom door as she lifted her hand and knocked lightly.

"Come in."

She entered, looking shyly at Luke Thomason. He was propped up on the pillow, staring at the dresser.

"Do you believe that verse?" he asked in a low, toneless voice.

Suzanne saw that he was looking at the Bible verse her mother had done in calligraphy and framed.

"All things work together for good for those who love the Lord," she repeated, placing the tray on the nightstand. "I admit I've had occasions to wonder, but then I always come back to trusting God. It's all I can do."

"It's a noble thought," he drawled. There was no mistaking the sarcasm that dripped from his words.

Suzanne glanced covertly at his handsome face, and noticed that the muscles in his jaw were clenched as he avoided her face. This time he was staring at the ceiling.

"You don't agree?" she asked gently.

"I won't say that I disagree." He closed his eyes. "My mother was religious."

"Yes, mine was as well. She died this winter."

"I'm sorry to hear that," he said quietly, still staring at the ceiling.

"Thank you." She opened her mouth to ask about his mother, then pressed her lips together. He obviously didn't want to talk to her, so there was no point in trying to be friendly.

"Call me when you're finished," she said.

He ignored the food as he continued to stare at the ceiling. She turned to go.

"Thank you," he said quietly as she reached the door.

She glanced back over her shoulder. He had turned his

head on the pillow, and was trying to force a smile as he looked at her. But all that followed was a mere twitch of his lips. Suzanne let a slow, wide smile spread over her lips. *There, let him see how it's done,* she thought.

"You're welcome," she said brightly.

He merely stared at her, saying nothing more. She walked out of the room, leaving him to ponder whatever had him so deep in thought.

⁂

"Everything all right?" Hank called from the porch as Suzanne hurried up the path from the stable the next afternoon.

"Everything's fine," she said, forcing a smile. In truth, the horses were almost out of feed, and their money was nearly gone.

Luke Thomason sat with her father on the porch. Luke looked rested and fresh in a change of clothes. She had left his belongings on the chair beside his bed, giving little thought to how he would manage to dress himself with only one hand. Apparently, he had accomplished the task with no problem. The bandage on his left side made a bulk through his blue denim shirt, but leaving the buttons undone allowed space. All in all, however, he looked just fine. Even his hair, she noted, was damp from grooming; his face was clean, his eyes blue—deep blue. She didn't really care for mustaches, but on him it looked okay.

She looked away, yanking her torn gloves from her fingers, hoping her father wouldn't notice their ragged condition. Her boots moved faster up the path, as she eagerly sought the shade and comfort of the cabin.

While this was her first spring in southern Colorado, she hadn't imagined it would be this warm. Summer was early, she decided, rolling up her shirt sleeves. A leisurely bath at the creek, that's what she needed. Or at least a quick swim.

"Mr. Waters, I've had some experience with horses," Luke was saying. "Maybe I could help out before I leave."

Hank snorted. "'Pears to me you're in worse shape than I am."

"There's nothing wrong with my hands. I can—"

"We're fine," Suzanne spoke up, shoving her gloves in her back pocket. "We don't need any help."

"How'd the back forty look?" Hank asked quickly.

Suzanne glanced at her father and saw the look of warning on his face. While Hank himself could be abrupt, he didn't like that trait in his daughter.

Sorry, she said with her eyes. Her optimism had been drained beneath a blazing sun while her mind had toiled over what tomorrow would bring.

"Looked fine," she repeated the words she had spoken earlier. Pa had to be constantly reassured that the horses, the fences, even the prairie dogs could survive without his close supervision.

She pushed the trailing strands of hair back from her face, trying to ignore Luke Thomason, who had taken an interest in her, now that she looked like a field hand. Who could figure men? Her brief experience with Walter Haddock in Denver had thoroughly bored her. Nevertheless, when she spotted one that interested her, he was either a renegade or...married, she thought, remembering the wedding band in the stranger's saddlebag.

"On Monday, I'm riding over to the trading post to replenish some supplies," she said to Hank.

"I'm coming with you," he said, pressing a hand to his rib cage as he moved to stand up.

"Pa, I don't need you to come with me!"

Suzanne regretted the impatience in her tone, but she was getting sick and tired of trying to avoid arguments with Hank.

"I'm not questioning whether you need me or not. I'm questioning my sanity if I don't get on Rocky and ride. This is the last day I'm gonna hole up here in this cabin like a prisoner!" Hank called after her as she hurried inside.

Suzanne knew he was venting his frustration, and she took no offense.

The cool dimness of the cabin was a welcome change as she crossed the board floors to the kitchen. After oversleeping, she had bolted out to do chores, leaving the breakfast dishes unwashed. She stopped, staring now at those dishes, washed and draining on the rack. It was not Hank's habit to wash dishes. On the rare occasions that he did, he simply piled everything haphazardly to drain. These dishes were neatly stacked. Was it possible Luke Thomason had cleaned up the kitchen?

She removed her wide-brimmed hat, and stared at the frayed ends of the leather sweatband. The poor old hat, left by someone on a nail in the barn, had been a blessing to her fair skin, and she was glad someone had abandoned it. As her eyes drifted over the battered hat, she couldn't help wondering what Luke Thomason thought of it.

Recalling his nice black hat with the smooth leather sweatband, she merely shook her head in frustration and hooked the hat on its peg on the wall.

She headed for the water bucket, wondering why she had been so defensive, moments before. Well, she knew the answer to that. All morning, as she had ridden over the pasture, she'd kept seeing those volatile blue eyes, angry, sad, worried, indifferent. She had kept wondering about him—what kind of life he had come from in Kansas, what he was going to in Colorado Springs.

She dipped a gourd into the bucket of water, gulping greedily to drown the dust in her throat. Well, if the man was ready to leave, let him go. They didn't need one more mouth to feed when they were facing starvation themselves.

She found her eyes wandering to the small looking glass on the wall, and tilted her head for a better view of herself. An oval face held delicate features and a small mouth. The sunburn on her fair skin had finally deepened to a healthy glow, leaving only a peeling nose as a reminder. Golden ringlets of hair had turned white around her forehead, having escaped her hat and bleached out beneath the sun.

She took a step closer, inspecting her image curiously. Her brows arched outward on the end, as though she were about to voice the questions always bubbling up in her inquisitive mind. Altogether it was a pleasant face, if not beautiful. Her chin was too long, her cheeks too hollow. Or so it seemed to her.

The door banged behind her and she turned to see Luke, heading in her direction. He was looking at her with a serious expression on his face. She wondered what was on his mind.

"Your father has convinced me I need to stay on another day. I was wondering if you'd mind if I helped out at the stable. There's nothing I like better than working with animals. How many do you have?"

"We're down to four horses. We have one stud, Rocky, and three mares. One is about to foal. Incidentally, I put your stallion in a corral to himself. He and Rocky didn't seem to like the looks of one another."

"Your pa told me you took care of him. I appreciate that."

She nodded. "Thanks for your offer of help, but we can manage."

"I know you can," he snapped.

She stared at him, shocked by his rude tone. She was ready to give him a piece of her mind, when he lifted his right hand and raked through his thick dark hair, slowly shaking his head.

"Look," he said more civilly, "I've worked hard all my life. I can't lounge around the porch, doing nothing, while you work like a man. . ."

His remark had stung. "Well, I don't know about the ladies where you come from, but out here, a woman has to work in order to survive."

He crammed his hands in his pants pockets and began to pace the kitchen floor. She realized then how tall he was, over six feet, yet he was lean and muscular. Yes, he did know something about work, she decided, so let him get on with his work, and leave them in peace. She had enough problems without dealing with another man. And why did men always want to argue?

What kind of woman did he leave behind? she wondered suddenly. *One who argued back, or sat with her hands folded demurely in her lap, while he sulked or argued.* Automatically, her eyes dropped to his broad hands, and she had a fleeting vision of the wedding ring around his right finger. *Why isn't there a thin white line there, showing where the ring had been?*

"Please, let me help," he said, leveling those blue eyes down into her upturned face. "Otherwise, I'll be leaving."

"You shouldn't ride until that wound heals," she protested.

Blue eyes bored into gray ones. From the front porch, Hank began to cough. At the sound of her father's repeated coughing, Suzanne looked toward the window, the tension of the moment broken.

She took a drink of water, trying to calm her scattered thoughts. Why was she being so defensive? What was wrong with her? If he wanted to help, why couldn't she accept his help and be grateful for it?

"All right, you can help," she said on a sigh. "I'm sure Pa would be relieved."

Luke turned and glanced toward the porch.

"He told me he loves this ranch and begrudges every minute he's not on the back of a horse," he said more civilly.

"Yes, he does," Suzanne responded.

A tightness clamped her throat as she fought against the sudden unexpected threat of tears. How could her father cope with losing this place, and their four pitiful horses? They didn't have much, but Hank had pinned his hopes on making a go of it.

Nervous and anxious, she leaned against the cabinet needing to talk. She looked at this stranger, who probably didn't care one way or another and decided to be honest with him. She was getting tired of wailing her problems at Nellie's docile face.

"He was a cowhand when he met my mother in Denver," she said. "Ma's family owned a mercantile business, and he was persuaded to hang up his spurs and become a merchant. He was never happy. Ma used to say," she smiled, remembering, "that Pa loved horses more than he loved her. It wasn't true, of course."

Luke was staring down at her, listening thoughtfully. "But he stayed in the mercantile business?" he asked.

"Yes. He did."

"Then you should be thankful for that," he said flatly.

Bitterness edged his tone, an indifferent mask slipping over his face again.

She sauntered to the stove and shook the battered coffee pot to see if there was anything left. A slosh answered her question.

"We were thankful," she said, heating the coffee. "But Ma wanted him to be happy. That's why she let her brother take advantage of them."

"What do you mean? Or maybe I shouldn't ask."

She shrugged. "My uncle was a dreamer, always chasing after get-rich-quick schemes. He never helped out in the family business. Finally Ma and Pa bought out his share after her parents died. Then, when he'd squandered everything, he came back to Denver with a real deal for them! He'd trade his horse ranch here for their share of the mercantile business. Pa jumped at the chance to have a small ranch, to go back to horses." She sighed. "It was a sorry bargain, but we've made the best of it."

"Made the best of it?" he echoed. "Why didn't your pa go back and thrash the daylights out of him?"

Suzanne laughed. "I guess Pa felt like doing that, but..." Her eyes swept over the living room, seeing in her mind's eye their nice living room in Denver: a room filled with Victorian furnishings, oil paintings, and Brussels carpets. That vision faded and she was looking at a horsehair couch, a straight-backed wooden chair, and a few plain end tables. A black iron stove and open shelves completed the kitchen. Only a few dishes and cooking utensils along with sparse cooking staples were visible on the shelves. Her gray eyes returned to the stranger in her kitchen. "My parents lived by Christian principles. They tried to believe that God had a reason for bringing them here."

"And what reason," he asked coldly, "did God have for

letting your mother die?"

The harshness of his tone stunned her as much as the cruel question he had asked. She stared for a moment, shocked to the core. Before she could summon a reply, however, he had turned and stridden out of the room, back to the porch. Her eyes followed him through the door, as he bounded down the steps, his right hand extended over his wounded shoulder, as though to protect it. But there seemed no way to protect, or to heal, the terrible wound he carried in his heart. And she began to suspect that wound had nothing to do with the bullet.

six

Luke had gone for a walk, ending up down behind the house near a stream. He propped his shoulder against a cottonwood trunk and allowed the spring breeze to soothe his frustration.

He had no right to speak to her that way, he knew it. But he was getting sick of hearing them pour out all their goodness and mercy. They were living in another world, not the real one.

Maybe they were just being nice to him, hoping he would stay on and work for them for free. Their price for saving his life. He lifted a broad hand and plowed through his thick hair. If only he had some money to give them, but he had nothing.

He recalled how he had been suckered in at the Godfrey ranch. William Godfrey had been a decent man, generous with his ranch hands, and kind to Luke. Then Amanda Godfrey, the old maid daughter, had set her eyes and her hopes on him, and all the trouble had started. She had been determined to have him, and she really thought it would be easy to hook him. She'd even told him so.

He sighed and began to walk toward the corral where he spotted Smoky, prowling restlessly. He hadn't figured Mr. Godfrey would go back on his word, but then blood was thicker than water, as Ma used to say.

He looked back at the Waters' cabin and wondered if they were setting that kind of trap for him. They seemed like kind, decent folks, but so had the Godfreys.

No, he couldn't take any chances. He'd help them out for a day or two, he owed them that. Then he'd find a job along the route to Colorado Springs. He could get a job; he'd been working since he was twelve years old.

"Hey, boy," he called to his horse.

The big horse trotted to the fence, thrusting his head forward to nuzzle Luke.

"Glad to see me, aren't you?"

He stroked the horse's gleaming coat, looking him over. "Looks like someone's taking care of you all right. We'll be leaving soon. We don't stay cramped up long, do we?"

He drew a deep breath of fresh air into his lungs, enjoying the smell of evergreen that mingled on the breeze. He wouldn't lose his temper again; he wouldn't insult her. He had no right. But she got to him as no other woman had. He couldn't stop looking at her, and now she was popping up in his thoughts when he should be thinking of more important things. Like remembering the reason he was headed to Colorado Springs.

*

Sundays had always been special days for Suzanne and her parents. In Denver most of their Sundays had been the same: church services followed by large Sunday dinners where family and friends gathered to enjoy food and fellowship. While their surroundings had changed drastically when they had taken up ranch life, one thing had not changed. Sundays were days of worship.

In the beginning, Suzanne's mother had simply brought out the family Bible and read scripture. Sometimes they sang a hymn, other times they prayed quietly. Then, Iva Parkinson had come calling, inviting them to Trails End on Sunday for a service held on the front porch of their ranch home. Soon that had become the tradition for the community.

At first it had been difficult for Hank and Suzanne to go to Trails End Ranch without Abigail. But after that first dreadful Sunday, when they'd spent the day mourning Abigail, Hank had informed Suzanne that her mother would expect them to go to worship. Missing Abigail more than ever the next Sunday, they had dressed and gone to Trails End to join in community worship and had not missed a Sunday since.

"Will you be going over to the Parkinson's ranch today?" Hank asked as Suzanne stood at the stove, stirring the breakfast gravy.

She yawned. "Yes, but I think you could be excused."

"I think so, too," he quickly agreed.

Suzanne smiled. If she had suggested that he go, he would have joined her, but she thought it was best for him to stay home. "I'll tell them you'll be back next week," she said.

He glanced toward the closed door of the bedroom. "Luke is sleeping late."

Luke! Suzanne's fingers stiffened as she popped open a biscuit and spread gravy over it. She had not told her father the vicious words the man had spoken yesterday. He had avoided her ever since, and she was glad for that. She knew how to apply alcohol and cotton and bandage to an outer wound. But this man had something festering in his soul. It would take a mightier power than she to heal that kind of wound, but Luke Thomason didn't want to read their verses or hear anything about the love of God.

She sat down at the table, nibbling on a small biscuit. She had left a larger one on the stove, in case their grumpy guest decided he was hungry. She glanced across the table at Pa. *He is strangely quiet this morning, suspiciously quiet,* she thought.

"What time is it?" she asked.

He withdrew the gold watch Ma had given him and studied the numerals on its face.

"Eight o'clock."

"I'd better get dressed."

Later, as she hurried through the living room, grabbing up her Bible, she met Luke's stare from the bedroom door.

"Good morning," he said, his tone cool, reserved.

His hair was neatly combed and his face bore evidence of a recent shave. The mustache was gone. She liked his face even better without the mustache.

"Good morning," she said.

He was looking her up and down, his eyes lingering on the front of her dress. Was something wrong, she wondered, glancing down to see if she had popped a button. No. The dress looked pretty enough, all cleaned and pressed. She loved the color—blue like a spring sky—and it complimented her gold hair and gray eyes.

Her eyes returned to him, and now he was staring at her hair. Suzanne lifted a hand, absently smoothing the hair net covering the chignon she wore today. Why was he looking at her that way? Then it came to her: this was the first time he had seen her in a dress, rather than pants and a shirt. *Doing a man's work! Hadn't that been his expression?*

She felt her cheeks burn as he continued to stare at her, and a wave of indignation swept her. He had a wife somewhere; he had no right looking at her like that, making her feel self-conscious. It was time to put the man in his place.

"Mr. Thomason, could I ask you something?"

"What is it?"

"Are you married?"

His dark brows arched at her bold question. No doubt, he was wondering what had prompted her question. She held herself erect, her eyes never wavering from his face.

"No."

A simple word that told her nothing.

She opened her mouth to ask about the wedding band, then just as quickly she pressed her lips together. She couldn't bring herself to mention the ring; perhaps it was pride. She didn't want him to think she had been pilfering through his things. Actually, she had been looking for some identification, but there was no point in explaining that now.

"I left breakfast on the stove," she said, hurrying through the front door.

❧

The spring morning was warm, but not uncomfortable, as Suzanne cantered Nellie toward Trails End Ranch, as puzzled as ever about Luke Thomason. Then suddenly she solved the mystery of Luke and the wedding band. His wife had died! Of course. That was why he was so mad at the world, so angry and bitter. Her heart began to soften, and by the time she joined the small group assembled on the wide porch of the rambling ranch house and joined in singing "Rock of Ages," she had forgotten her troubles.

Arthur Parkinson, Jr., a tall young man of twenty who still had not grown into his hands and feet, slipped into the chair beside Suzanne. He turned to grin at her, and she smiled politely, never missing a word of the hymn.

Why couldn't she feel something more than friendship for Art, she wondered as his pale blue eyes kept sneaking in her direction. He was nice, polite, well mannered. Single. And rich, Pa had reminded her. As the only son of the largest landowner in the area, Art had something to offer.

She sidled a glance at him. He sang in a clear tenor, but she didn't like the way his Adam's apple always bobbed against his collar. In fact, it was the largest Adam's apple she'd ever seen.

She turned her attention to Arthur Parkinson, Senior, a tall, distinguished-looking man in his fifties. He stood with his Bible, ready to read scripture. She could see a vague resemblance between father and son; unfortunately, Art looked more like his mother. Suzanne scolded herself for the thought. Mrs. Parkinson was very nice—and she couldn't help it if her eyes bulged just a bit.

⁂

Suzanne had settled Nellie in the corral, rewarding her with a handful of oats from the dwindling supply, and headed to the house. She had spotted Pa and Luke on the porch as she turned up the path. From the way Pa's mouth was moving, she figured he had filled Luke Thomason's head this morning.

Once she reached the house, she saw it was Luke who was doing the talking. Hank, for once, was doing the listening.

"My grandfather bought land and cattle from the Mexicans in southeast Texas," Luke was saying. "He was an immigrant who came west with only a few dollars in his pockets."

"So did he get rich?" Hank inquired.

Again that pause that Suzanne had come to expect from Luke when questioned about a personal matter.

"No, he went broke. And he drifted north to Kansas."

"What happened there?" Hank asked, conversationally.

"He died a pauper."

An awkward silence followed. Then Hank turned to his daughter. "Did you pray for us, daughter?"

"Of course," she replied, allowing her smile to extend from her father to Luke for a brief moment. "Mrs. Parkinson was in true form this morning, missing all the high notes to 'Rock of Ages'."

Hank laughed heartily, appreciating her humor, but Luke's mouth merely twitched.

"And did Art sneak a seat beside you?" Hank demanded good naturedly, winking at Luke. "Parkinson's son has a crush on Suzanne."

"Pa!" she reprimanded sharply, lifting her skirt to plant a kid leather slipper on the slab log step.

Slowly, her eyes slid to Luke as she reminded herself that she had asked God to forgive her for being so judgmental of the man. She was going to be more patient with him.

As Suzanne continued to the porch, Luke came to his feet. She might object to his grumpiness at times, but he had offered to help around the house. She supposed that he did have nice manners. She appreciated that. Her mother has always told her to seek a man with manners.

"Are you men hungry?" she asked.

"I could eat," Hank answered.

"No, I'm not hungry at all," Luke replied, turning his blue eyes toward the distant mountain range.

Good, Suzanne thought, *I won't have to add more gravy to the last of the venison roast.* She entered the house, humming "Rock of Ages," determined to hold onto her good mood for the rest of the day.

Luke Thomason proved to be more hungry than he'd thought, for after Hank nagged him into submission, he had joined them at the table. At first, he seemed to feel awkward and out of place—particularly when Suzanne said grace—but he began to relax as Hank broached the subject of rodeos.

"Yes, sir. I made most of my money rodeoing on weekends."

"Ever get hurt?" Hank asked.

"Just once. Nothing serious." He had glanced at Suzanne, who immediately pretended an interest in filling the water glasses. She had a feeling if he had broken both legs he'd never admit it. He was determined to appear as healthy as his horse.

"I've been meaning to ask," she whirled, water pitcher in hand. "What's your horse's name? I hate not being able to call him by his name when I talk to him..."

She had just given herself away. Her delight in petting the stallion, and imagining the life he and his master lived, had been her own secret until now. Now they knew she was in the habit of talking to animals!

"His name is Smoky. When people look at him, they wonder where I got the name."

"He has a smoky-looking patch on his forehead," Suzanne guessed. "I think it's a very good name."

Luke half smiled. "You're right about the patch. That's where he got his name."

"And my bay is named after these wonderful mountains."

"Rocky." Luke nodded. "That too is a good name."

"But not as good as Nellie," Suzanne countered, enjoying the conversation now. She filled each glass, set the pitcher down, and took her seat again.

"And since we're comparing names," Luke said, "how did you settle on Nellie?"

Suzanne hesitated, glancing at her father. His gray eyes were amused as he looked across the table at her, obviously curious to see how she would answer.

"Because it suits her," she said with a smile. "And because that was her name when we bought her, sick, half starved, and half price, from a desperate rancher's wife."

It had turned into a pleasant meal. Luke had offered to help with the dishes but she had refused. Pa had gone to the sofa; Luke had wandered off somewhere, and Suzanne had dragged to her bed as soon as the kitchen was clean. Sunday had always been a day of rest for them, and today she was looking very forward to a long nap.

She was almost asleep when her father's voice echoed through the house.

"Suzanne!"

She heard the urgency in his tone and jumped out of bed, pulling an everyday dress on over her petticoats and chemise.

"Suzanne!" His voice came from the porch. "Hurry."

She bolted from her room, reaching the front door just in time to see Hank fall in the yard. He landed face down on the ground, yelping in disgust as he tried to lift his ankle.

"What are you doing?" she cried.

"What does it look like I'm doing?" he snapped. "I was trying to get to the stable. . ."

"Pa, you know you can't go down there. The path is filled with gopher holes and you could turn your ankle again. But you just did! What am I going to do with you?" she cried in frustration.

"Will you quit babbling and listen to me?" Hank snapped, glaring at her. "Something's wrong with one of the horses. Hurry!" He bit the words out through clenched teeth as one hand shot to his rib cage. She wondered if he'd cracked another rib.

Suzanne leaped to her feet and saw Luke bounding out the door of the house. His eyes shot from Suzanne to Hank sprawled on the ground.

"Help him!" She cried as she tore out to the stable.

She could hear the cries of an animal in pain, and her heart jumped to her throat. She tried not to think about what she would find. From the animal's shrill cry she envisioned a grizzly in the barn, tearing into the mare's flesh...

She burst through the door of the stable, blinking against the dimness, giving no thought to what she would have done if, in fact, a grizzly *had* been loose in the barn. Instead, she came up short, her nose tingling from the tartness of straw and manure...and the mare in labor!

Blaze was down in the clean straw that Suzanne had lovingly provided the day before, her bulging abdomen heaving with the struggle of giving birth.

"Oh, Blaze," Suzanne cried, rushing to the narrow stall.

She dropped down beside the brown mare and ran her palm up and down the white star on the mare's forehead. Like her father, Suzanne kept a special place in her heart for the horses. What if there was a complication, what if . . . . The horror of losing Blaze was more than Suzanne could bear.

The mare rolled her head, peering up at Suzanne with wild, pain-filled eyes. She seemed to be begging for help, and feeling more helpless than ever, Suzanne sank her teeth in her lower lip. Of all times for her father to be laid up! He would know exactly what to do here, while Suzanne's knowledge was limited to comforting words. Why hadn't they discussed this, she wondered, as her frustration turned to panic.

The stable door creaked and she whirled to see Luke hurrying back to the stall. A wave of relief swept over her, even though she knew his assistance was limited to one good arm. He said nothing as he looked grimly at the mare. She needed desperately to hear something encouraging, but she doubted she would hear anything very encouraging from this man, who seemed to see only the dark side.

He knelt down beside the mare, using his right hand to gently prod her side. Then he moved to the mare's bottom to appraise the situation.

"The colt is coming," he announced matter-of-factly. "Do you have any instruments for. . ."

"Pa has a black bag up at the house."

"Please get it," he said, as he stretched out his right hand to gently stroke the mare's heaving side. "And tell him we can manage."

Could they? she wondered during her flight from the stable to the house. Hank, huddled on the porch step, was firing questions as fast as he could speak.

"Blaze is in labor," she said, rushing past him.

From inside she grabbed the black bag and a towel from the cupboard, then ran breathlessly for the stable.

Suzanne thrust the bag and towel toward Luke, then crumpled down, gasping for breath. She saw that Luke had managed to get both shirt sleeves rolled up, preparing for his role as veterinarian. Her eyes fell to his broad hand, his smooth long fingers, and her confidence was strengthened. Nevertheless, she felt compelled to ask the question that had popped into her mind during her frantic run.

"Have you ever done this?"

"Of course," he answered tersely.

Well, how did she know? She had a right to ask, didn't she? He shot a brief glance in her direction. "The mare does most of the work anyway," he added.

"Oh." She took a deep breath, trying to calm her nerves. She had no choice but to trust him; on the other hand, he could be a Godsend.

"Try to keep her still," Luke instructed.

Suzanne placed her hand on the mare's neck and began to murmur words of comfort.

"It's okay," she spoke softly. "We're going to help you get the little one here."

The mare whinnied and made an effort to get up. Suzanne clung to her and began to chatter, saying whatever came to mind.

"We're halfway there," Luke called to her.

His voice floated over Blaze's suffering body, and she thought the man sounded calm, in control. Suddenly she was very glad to have him here with her, doing the work, helping Blaze. Maybe she could put up with his grumpiness a little while longer.

The mare tossed her head back and bared her teeth in a moan of anguish. "Hang on, sweetie," she said, wrapping her arms around the mare's neck, "it's almost over."

"It *is* over," Luke spoke confidently.

Suzanne looked across at him. A gleam of perspiration filled his handsome face, but the blue eyes glowed with pride. For the first time, a broad smile softened that serious mouth. "We have a hearty little male."

"*We do?*" Suzanne squealed, alarming the mare with her outburst. "I'm sorry, Blaze. I didn't mean to startle you, but you have a healthy baby."

The mare heaved one long quivering sigh and sank into the straw, as though she understood what Suzanne had said.

Suzanne unwound her arms from the mare and crawled around to Luke. He was wrapping a towel around the colt and Suzanne stared, feeling a wave of tenderness sweep over her.

"Could I hold him?"

"Careful," Luke instructed, placing the warm wiggling bundle in her arms.

Suzanne touched the miniature blaze on his forehead. "He's just like his mother. Luke, he's the most beautiful creature I've ever seen," she said.

Luke grinned. "Yeah, he is."

She turned to Luke, smiling warmly. "I don't know how to thank you."

"Seeing the healthy colt is thanks enough," he said, trailing a finger down the colt's forehead. "I've always felt that animals are much kinder than people. I like helping them."

Suzanne opened her mouth to ask just why he felt that way, but something restrained her. He was such a private person, revealing so little about himself.

"I guess we should give him to his mother now," Luke said, "if you can bear to part with him."

Reluctantly, she handed over the colt, and Luke placed him next to Blaze. Suzanne watched, admiring how adeptly Luke managed with only his right hand. She wondered how soon he would be leaving. He had just proven he could fare for himself. He had also proven how desperate they were for help here.

A heaviness tugged at her heart as she stood, brushing the straw from her dress. "I'll go deliver the news to Pa. He's probably crawling down the path to the stable."

She was surprised to hear Luke chuckle. So he was capable of laughter, after all.

"Then let me go meet him," Luke smiled as he trotted out the door.

Suzanne's heart was full of joy as she looked back at the new colt. She laughed as he searched eagerly for his first meal.

"Suzanne?" Luke called as she reached the door of the barn.

She turned, startled to hear her name on his lips. She hadn't been sure he even remembered it. She looked up as he came running down the path.

"Your pa has turned his ankle again, and he may have injured his ribs as well."

"Oh, no! I don't know what I'm going to do with him!"

"Can't you find another ranch hand? You've got to have some help here." Again that irritable tone had crept back to his voice.

"Good help is hard to come by," she said, quoting Hank. Pride kept her from admitting the truth: there was no money for extra help. The only way they could survive was to do the work themselves. And even so, she was beginning to wonder how much longer they could hold on.

She looked at Luke and decided to be forthright. "Maybe we could work something out with you."

He shook his head, looking away. "I have to be on my way soon."

"Oh, well." She turned her eyes toward the door, trying to conceal her disappointment. "It was just a thought. Anyway, maybe the colt is a good sign," she called over her shoulder then hurried out.

As she rushed up the path to check on Pa and tell him the good news, she thought again of the sturdy little colt. Sharing something so special had made her realize how lonely she was. She longed to share the joys and tears of life with someone besides her father.

She thought about Luke Thomason, wondering if there was some way they could persuade him to stay on. Even with a bandaged arm, he was far better help than any of the other drifters who hung around the post. He seemed so eager to leave, but maybe, just maybe, he would change his mind.

❧

Luke stared after Suzanne, turning the words she had spoken over and over in his mind. Maybe he had been wrong about her and her pa trying to sucker him into staying. If they were laying a trap for him, she wouldn't have been so nice about it when he'd said he was leaving. Would she?

He turned back to the little colt, smiling as he reached forward to gently touch him. The last hour had brought a warm and tender feeling to his heart. He was relieved to know he could still have such a feeling.

He sighed, leaning back against the straw, thinking about Suzanne again. With straw in her hair and perspiration on her upper lip, she was as appealing as ever. Her eyes had radiated such tenderness and love for the colt. He closed his eyes, wondering how he would feel if she had looked at him that way.

His eyes snapped open. Well, she wouldn't. As for trying to snag him for a husband, the rich rancher—Parkinson, was it?—was the one she was after. Why else would someone go all the way to another ranch for a worship service? It surprised him even more that Mr. Waters was accustomed to going with her.

He snorted. Parkinson didn't have a chance against both of them!

seven

Suzanne had sneaked quietly into the kitchen and removed the tin can from the top shelf of the cupboard. She didn't want Hank asking any questions. It occurred to her that she was having to sneak around her father a lot lately, but her intentions were good, and for the time being, he needed to be protected.

The tin can served as a bank for their cash. Each time she pulled the can down, it felt lighter and lighter. Today, it practically toppled from her hands. She closed her eyes for a moment, praying she had miscounted yesterday. Surely a couple of bills had been stuck together.

Please, God, she silently prayed as she sucked in her breath and gently eased the lid up. Her hopes sank. Only a few bills nestled in the bottom of the can. She had to think of something! She was no horse trader, but even if she were, Hank had put his foot down. He would hire on as a ranch hand over at Bar X, or mop floors at the trading post before another horse left their pasture.

What alternatives were left? She had never relished the idea of raising pigs or chickens, but she supposed she could learn. And that vegetable garden would have to be a reality now. She could learn anything she put her mind to; besides, what could be so hard about planting seeds in the ground, then watering and weeding?

That simple question prompted a glance out the kitchen window, and she knew there was nothing simple about a vegetable garden.

After much deliberation, she took half the money. She had no choice. The flour and sugar bins were empty, and Pa couldn't survive without his coffee. She'd grown adept at re-using coffee grounds, but there was no point in trying to serve thin brown water.

She sighed. Somehow, a way would be provided. She heard Luke's voice from the front porch and prayed he would change his mind about leaving. He was big and strong, obviously a hard worker, and he seemed to know a lot about horses. Two days had passed since they had worked side by side, delivering the colt. He hadn't mentioned leaving, and she had tiptoed around the subject. Since she had given him the job of feeding the animals, he seemed to take particular delight in his trips down to the stable, checking on Blaze and her colt. He was even offering to ride over the range on his black stallion, but Hank had balked at that.

"Back in my years, I tore open a wound bouncing around in the saddle. You gotta give yourself a couple more days," he had admonished Luke.

She turned back to the bills crumpled in her palm, and thrust them into her drawstring purse, along with the list she had spent hours devising. Only the bare essentials, and those trimmed even further.

Looping her purse strings over her arm, she headed for the front door. She was grateful that at last Pa had someone with whom to discuss land and horses—his favorite subjects. At least, this had kept him on the porch and off the back of Rocky. The rangy bay prowled his pen restlessly, as eager as his master to be streaking across the back forty. Maybe she'd ask Luke to exercise him tomorrow, if he felt up to it. Her eyes darted from Luke to her father as she stepped onto the porch.

"I'm riding over to the trading post for some supplies," she announced. "Also, I'm leaving word for Doc Browning to stop by when he makes the route." She looked at Luke. "It would be a good idea for him to see you too."

"I'm doing fine. Anyway, I'll be leaving soon," he added, looking away.

Those words were like a pinprick in her lungs, deflating all the air. She hadn't realized how much she had hoped, even depended, on him staying on until Pa was better.

Suzanne glanced at her father, thinking how little he knew about the tin can and its dwindling contents. Still, she was pleased to note that he looked cheerful this morning. His gray hair was neatly combed, his beard trimmed, and those gray eyes, faded by the sun and wind, looked rested.

"Luke tells me the colt's doing fine," Hank said.

Suzanne smiled. "Yes, he is."

She started down the steps and saw, to her amazement, that Nellie was already saddled and waiting. She whirled on Hank, ready to fuss at him.

"Hope you don't mind," Luke spoke up. "When your father mentioned you were going into town, I took the liberty of saddling your mare."

"But your shoulder. . . ?"

"I'm okay," he said, frowning at her. He seemed to take offense whenever she questioned his health, so she made up her mind never to mention it again.

"Well, you ain't up to riding all the way to Colorado Springs," Hank said gruffly.

Suzanne glanced sharply at her father. He liked having Luke around; that was obvious.

"Pa, we don't want to detain him when he's ready to leave."

Hank withdrew his pipe from his pocket, saying nothing

more.

It was nice to have Nellie all saddled up and ready to go. She was glad Luke had saved her the time and effort. But they could get along without him, she reminded herself stoutly.

"Well, I'll be back in a couple of hours."

"You take care, missy," Hank called after her.

"I can do that better than you," she yelled back.

She mounted sidesaddle, waved to the men, and trotted Nellie down the road to Wiley's Post. Miles of level land stretched around her, bordered by the far flung fences of Bar X, the biggest ranch in the area. Three smaller ranches made up the remaining territory before the terrain climbed to the Pikes Peak foothills.

It was a big robust land, and she could see why Hank had been so eager to settle here. Yet, this life was hard, requiring so much from them. It wouldn't be a bad life, if only their circumstances were different.

"God is our refuge and strength, she told herself. She followed that one up with, *All things work together for good. . ."*

Suzanne recalled Luke's suggestion of a ranch hand. Their one experience with hired help had been a disaster. Wally had been a drinker who was undependable and lazy, finally deserting them during a January blizzard. Quickly, she turned her eyes toward a cottonwood thicket, attempting to thwart the memory of the three of them—Pa, Ma, and herself—out, trying to get the horses rounded up. That night Ma had started running a fever and died before Doc Browning could get through the deep snow to see her.

Suzanne prodded her mind back to the present as she cantered Nellie up to the log-post rail. She always enjoyed chatting with Mattie, who managed to make everyone who came around feel better. She slipped down from Nellie and looped the reins around the log hitching rail. She hurried across the plank porch and pressed down the latch of the wide door.

Inside, half a dozen elk and moose racks overhung a blackened stone fireplace in a huge room. The front of the store was devoted to shelves and counters crammed with an assortment of general merchandise. At the rear, a long table, with two adjoining benches, served as dining table for the meals Mattie served to hungry customers. Two cowboys hunched over their coffee cups. Their felt hats sat low on their foreheads, and their range clothes were dusty and wrinkled.

Mary, Suzanne's best friend from Denver, had written letters inquiring if she had found herself a handsome cowboy. "You haven't seen *these* cowboys," Suzanne had written back.

"Well, look who's here," Mattie's strong voice rose above the clatter of dishes.

Suzanne hurried back to the kitchen, a small room filled to bursting, containing an iron cook stove, narrow shelves and counters, and dry goods stacked halfway up the wall.

"Hi, Mattie!" Suzanne called to the woman who was elbow deep in a dish pan overflowing with soap suds. The sight of Mattie made Suzanne feel better.

"I've been wondering when you'd come over for a visit," Mattie said, grabbing a cup towel to dry her hands.

Standing five feet ten inches tall, Mattie was the epitome of the sturdy pioneer woman. She joked that she wouldn't serve folks food she hadn't first tasted, and folks laughed with her and thought nothing of her extra pounds. Her fifty odd years were written boldly in her round face, yet her brown eyes still held a youthful sparkle. The flavor of cinnamon drifted from her muslin apron and calico dress, and Suzanne found that comforting. Her thick brown hair, sprinkled with gray, was drawn into a bun.

"How's your pa?" she asked.

"As cranky as ever. I need the doc to come by and check on him. He had a bad fall this week."

Mattie looked concerned. "Doc Browning will be at Trails End tomorrow morning. They're having a meeting of cattlemen about a drive to Pueblo. He'll check in after the meeting, and I'll send him over. Anything else I can do?"

"No, Luke's keeping him company."

"Luke?" Mattie arched a brow.

It occurred to Suzanne that nobody knew about their strange guest.

"Yes, there's a man—"

"Stage is here," one of the cowboys yelled.

The arrival of the stage twice a week was a major event at the post, prompting Mattie into a frenzy. Mattie brushed past Suzanne with a force that nearly toppled her, had she not grabbed a chair for support, and then she hurried after Mattie.

Like everyone else, Suzanne was curious about the stage and its passengers. Mattie jerked the door open, admitting the sound of thudding hoofbeats and jingling harness. Driver and team were engaged in a battle of strength, and Suzanne began to wonder who would win. When finally the horses had been wrestled to a halt, and the violently-rocking stage had settled, the driver leaned back in the seat, planted a dusty boot on the brake, and tipped his frayed hat at Mattie.

"You're losing ground, Willie!" Mattie laughed.

"I was just teasing Robert," he said, baring tobacco-stained teeth in a wide grin as he turned to his companion, a young cowboy who served as shotgun messenger.

The younger man, not amused, dropped down and hobbled to the stage door, yanking it open. Dust cascaded like a waterfall before he unfolded the iron steps.

Two men, hats askew, tugged irritably at their rumpled clothing as they stumbled down the steps and stared bleary-eyed at the log trading post.

"Got any coffee?" Willie yelled.

"Always got coffee," Mattie motioned them inside. "Tom, put that bottle away," she admonished one of the cowboys at the table. "You know my rules. No drinking."

She turned back to the strangers, entering the post. "You men come inside. I've got beef stew and coffee."

Suzanne trailed after Mattie. "Can I help?"

Mattie, in full stride to the kitchen, merely smiled at Suzanne's offer. "No thanks, honey. I have everything under control, believe it or not."

"I believe it," Suzanne replied, watching in amazement as Mattie poured coffee, dipped stew, and dispensed utensils all at once. And she did it with grace. "I'll just gather up the supplies I need," Suzanne said feebly, aware that nobody was paying her any attention.

She took her time, sauntering around the store, pricing every item.

"Can you find what you need?" Mattie asked, joining her after the men were served.

"Oh, sure. Mattie, don't you need some help here? You seem awfully busy," Suzanne tried to keep her tone casual. She didn't want Mattie to know how desperate they were.

"My sister Lilly is coming soon."

"Is that right?" Suzanne smiled. "Well, I know you'll be

glad to have her with you."

Mattie's husband had died the previous year, and Suzanne often wondered how Mattie could possibly do all the work. Yet she did, while maintaining a thriving business and keeping errant cowboys under control.

"Well, you got everything?" Mattie came around behind the board counter and looked at Suzanne.

"I think so. Mattie, I'd like to have a vegetable garden this year. When you have time, could you give me some pointers? You raise lots of vegetables, don't you?"

"I try, but the soil is not as good here as it was back in Dallas." She heaved a sigh. "It's hard work." She paused, as her brown eyes swept Suzanne. "I might just ride over to your place once Lilly comes to relieve me; I could take a look at the soil, tell you what might grow best. And maybe I'll argue a bit with your old man."

Something in the way Mattie spoke those words rang a bell in the back of Suzanne's mind. She recalled seeing Mattie and her pa in a spirited political debate around the pot-bellied stove one winter day. Both had defended their opinions with fiendish delight. Pa had thoroughly enjoyed it.

"Where'd the stranger come from who's staying at your place?" Mattie asked.

"Kansas. He's on his way to Colorado Springs." She frowned. "He made the mistake of stopping in Bordertown and getting in a poker game. A poor loser followed him up the trail, shot, and robbed him. He managed to make it to our valley. I spotted him just before he fell off his horse."

Mattie's mouth fell open. "You don't say? What about the culprit who shot him?"

"He got away."

"A poker game," Mattie said, shaking her head. "There's

usually a gun battle afterwards. Too bad."

"But Luke isn't really a gambler."

Suzanne recognized the defensive tone in her voice as soon as she had spoken the words. And so had Mattie, whose brown eyes swung to Suzanne with a look of suspicion.

"Young lady, do we need to have a talk?"

Suzanne waved the suggestion aside. "No, he's leaving in a day or so. He's in a big hurry to get to Colorado Springs," Suzanne said, hoping to avoid a lecture from Mattie.

"What does this fellow look like?" she asked.

"Tall, with black hair and blue eyes."

Mattie planted her elbows firmly on the counter and leaned forward. "Tall, dark, and handsome," Mattie said, eyeing Suzanne.

"Don't get any ideas," Suzanne scolded.

Mattie laughed. "Why not? I'm an old romantic, you know. I don't have a husband any more, so I just have to enjoy listening to someone else talk about a handsome man. . . ."

"I didn't say handsome; you did!"

"But I believe you think so," Mattie grinned.

Suzanne opened her purse. "How much do I owe you?"

Mattie turned and began to tally the items Suzanne had lined up on the counter.

Suzanne waited, growing more nervous with each figure Mattie added to her tablet. Mattie would let her charge, but still. . . .

When Mattie gave her the sum, Suzanne stared at the figures. *That wasn't so bad, after all.*

Suzanne cleared her throat. "Did you add everything? I thought I would owe more."

Mattie grinned. "The good Lord looks out for us."

Suzanne nodded, counting out her money. She still had some change to spare. "Yes, He does. That's one thing I know for sure."

Mattie packaged the supplies while Suzanne said her good-byes and started for the door. The young stagehand rushed up. "Ma'am, let me help you with those packages."

"Why, thank you," she said, smiling at him.

He was polite and sort of handsome, she thought. Maybe it was time she started looking for a husband to help her and Pa run the ranch.

As she tied her bundle onto the saddle horn and waved to the young man, she decided he looked too young to be considered husband material. She sighed, digging her heels into Nellie's side. Maybe she was one of those women who were meant to remain single, although she had always longed for children and a husband who would look at her the way Pa had looked at Ma.

She sighed again, staring across the wide valley to the blazing sunset unfolding on the horizon. To her consternation, she found herself thinking of Luke Thomason again.

She arrived back at the ranch just as the evening shadows had begun to stretch over the valley. Luke stood at the stable door, watching her ride up.

"Make the trip okay?" he asked almost pleasantly.

"Just fine."

He stepped forward and extended his hand as she placed her heel in the stirrup and swung down. His strong grip on her elbow was reassuring, and she smiled her appreciation as he assisted with her packages.

"Your father's feeling a little tired. I insisted on sleeping on the couch tonight so he could go back to his bed. Maybe he'll rest better."

Suzanne nodded, listening as he spoke, and thinking he was being a chatterbox compared to the reserve he normally displayed in her presence.

"I'm going to fetch Doc Browning tomorrow to have a look at Pa. He'll be at the cattlemen's meeting at Trails End in the morning."

"Trails End?"

"The Parkinson ranch that adjoins ours. The ranchers are organizing a cattle drive to Pueblo, and Doc's a cattleman." It was several seconds before Suzanne realized they were staring at each other. "Well," she said, looking away, "I'll go on to the house. Thanks for your help."

"You're welcome," he said, leading her mare into the stable.

Despite her weariness, Suzanne's spirits lifted as she sauntered up the path to the house. She paused along the way, glancing up at the pale stars already poking their heads through the blue curtain of sky. She took a deep breath of the fresh spring air, inhaling the flavor of the wildflowers blooming down behind the house.

She glanced back at the stable, hearing the sound of a bucket clanging as Luke tended to his chores. Encouraged by Luke's attitude, she decided things weren't really so bad after all. The colt *had* been a good sign.

Her soaring spirits crashed, however, when she walked through the front door and met Hank's angry face. He was seated at the kitchen table, staring down into the cookie tin.

"Why in the world did you spend so much money today?" he growled, eyeing her meager packages. "And what did you buy? Don't look like much."

Suzanne drew a deep breath, wishing she could have better prepared herself for this confrontation.

"I bought flour, sugar, and coffee. A few spices. That's

all."

"Horse feed? No horse feed?" he asked in disbelief.

"We have enough for another week—"

"Suzanne, I demand to know when you've spent all this money."

Suzanne set the packages on the table and faced him squarely. "Pa, the money has been dwindling all winter. Ma stretched every dollar, and I've done the same. You shouldn't have bought that last mare. . . ."

As the words tumbled out, she realized she had wanted to speak those words for weeks. Pa, as usual, had gotten carried away when it came to horses. His face flushed darkly as he came to his feet, flinched, then slumped back into the chair.

"How am I supposed to run a horse ranch without horses?" he demanded. "You and your ma want to spend all the money on—"

"On what?" Suzanne lashed out, furious now that he had not appreciated their frugality. "Food? Your coffee?"

He looked away, stung by her words. She knew she was inflicting more guilt, but he needed to understand her side of the matter. She should have discussed the situation with him sooner, rather than trying to protect him as Ma had.

"I can do without my coffee. And if our money's gone, I can do without food as well. I'm sending you back to Denver where you can have a decent life!"

"And that'll solve everything, won't it?" she cried. "Just how do you propose to send me back to Denver when we don't have enough money left to buy oats for the horses?"

As their argument raged, their voices growing louder, they failed to notice Luke Thomason standing in the front door. The board had creaked beneath his boot as he came to an abrupt halt. Suzanne whirled, her cheeks flaming.

Anger was replaced by humiliation when she realized the man had heard everything.

Seeing his error, he turned and headed back to the porch, leaving them to their battle.

Tears filled Suzanne's eyes as she turned and fled to her room. Why did she and her pa always get into a shouting match? Why couldn't life take a turn for the better? Every time she thought it had, something cropped up again, making the situation worse than before.

Tears poured down her cheeks as she bit her trembling lip and decided maybe the argument was a good thing. The truth was out in the open now. Let Pa decide what to do!

A soft knock sounded on the door.

"What is it?" she said, trying to steady her voice.

"Daughter, I'm sorry," Hank said through the closed door. "I know you've done the best you could."

Suzanne grabbed an old bandanna from her dresser and dabbed at her eyes. She couldn't stay mad upon hearing the humility in her father's voice. One thing about Pa, he was never too proud to apologize, and she loved him for that.

She sniffled and cracked open the door.

Hank's cheeks were damp too, and he seemed to have aged a few more years in the last ten minutes.

"I'm sorry too," she said, opening the door wider as his thin arms encircled her shoulders, drawing her to him.

"We'll make it," he said, hugging her hard.

Suzanne nodded. "I know." She hugged him back, trying to sound confident. Beneath her fingers, her father's jutting shoulder blades reminded her he had lost more weight. His voice, always so strong, now sounded faint. She bit her lip, no longer confident about anything.

eight

Suzanne rolled over in her bed, squinting up at the shaft of sunlight. What time was it? Had she overslept? She lay there for a moment, trying to analyze why this particular morning seemed different from all the others. She sat up on her elbow, listening. The air felt cold, stale, and the smell of fresh coffee was missing.

She tossed the covers back and grabbed her robe while shoving her feet into her worn house slippers. Remembering Luke Thomason was a guest here, she paused at the door, buttoning her robe all the way to her chin. Then she smoothed her hair back, cracked the door, and peered into the living room.

Luke was nowhere in sight. The blanket was folded neatly at the end of the sofa. Her eyes flew to the closed door of her father's bedroom. Had Pa refused to make coffee because they had argued over the money spent for it? No, he didn't hold grudges or stay mad. She tiptoed across the living room to her father's bedroom and gently turned the knob.

He was still in bed, lying on his side, facing the wall. It wasn't like him to stay in bed so late. Was something wrong? A sudden panic overtook her. The pain of losing her mother was still fresh in her heart. She couldn't begin to comprehend what losing Hank would mean. Her heart lunged to her throat and for a moment, she was paralyzed by fear. Her lips parted, but she couldn't force herself to call his name. What would she do if he didn't respond? Her eyes clung to his back as her breath froze.

His shoulders rose and fell, ever so slightly. He was breathing evenly; he was all right. She heaved a sigh, weak with relief. She remembered their argument, the worry over money. He'd probably not slept well.

She closed the door gently, not wanting to disturb him.

"Thank you, God," she said aloud, padding back across the living room. As long as Hank was alive, nothing seemed quite so bad. Passing the coffee table, she caught a flash of gold in the sunlight. She stopped, staring for several seconds before she realized what she was seeing. Slowly, she walked to the table and stared down at the wedding band, placed on a sheet of paper.

She sank onto the couch, not touching the ring or the paper, and sat there for a while. Then, drawing a deep breath, she reached forward, gently placing the wedding band on the table, and lifting the letter to read the masculine scrawl.

> *I can't thank you enough for saving my life and sharing your home and food with me. I'm leaving the only thing of value that I own. Maybe you can sell it and get some money to tide you over. Thanks for your help.*
>
> *Luke Thomason*

Suzanne lifted the gold wedding band and studied it thoughtfully. It was not shiny and new, but softly burnished and worn—lovingly worn, no doubt. She turned the ring over, inspecting the inner side as a miniature design caught her eye. Two dainty hearts were joined together, with each heart holding a tiny initial. G in one heart, L in the other.

Luke.

She stared into space, feeling numbness give way to disappointment. She glanced at the closed door of the bedroom, wondering how Hank would take the news that Luke had deserted them, just when they needed him most. As for the ring, where did he expect her to hock a wedding band?

She leaped from the sofa, pacing the floor. The man would rather part with this ring, a loving link to his wife, than put in a few days' work here, where he could see he was desperately needed!

Coward! She paced a wider circle, her steps moving quickly over the boards. She bit her lip, frustrated to tears, and another emotion battled her senses, frustrating her even more. She had been attracted to this man, and now she hated herself for it.

From the moment she'd found him, injured and bleeding to death, she had been struck by the fact that he was the most handsome man she'd ever seen. And later, as she had cleaned the wound, bound his shoulder, and prepared and served him food, she had felt drawn to him, despite his reserve which often bordered on rudeness.

Then she had decided he was a widower coming to Colorado Springs to forget the sorrow of losing his wife. She had wanted him to stay here with them, to bring the smile back to Hank's face, to help her through this difficult time.

Her pacing ended at the table as she stared dumbly at the ring, then the letter. She leaned down, folded the letter over the wedding band, and wandered into her bedroom to place both in a drawer.

No way would she sell a wedding band with two hearts joined together just to buy a sack of oats for the horses! The man knew very little about Wiley's Trading Post. Mattie needed cash, not a wedding band; Mattie already had one of those, and she would starve to death before she'd part with it. She couldn't barter a wedding band for a ranch hand, which was what they needed most.

She yanked down her work clothes from a shelf, unable to stem the frustration boiling through her. Of course she could sell gold in Colorado Springs, but she didn't have the money to get there!

"Suzanne. . . ."

"Coming," she called at the sound of her father's voice. She tugged on her clothes and hurried barefoot across the living room floor, poking her head into the bedroom.

"My chest is giving me some trouble this morning," Hank said, pushing himself up on the pillow. "Since you've got Luke to help you, maybe I'll just stay in bed a while longer."

"Good idea, Pa."

Never could she recall her pa staying in bed. The old fear rose in her anew as she walked to his bed and looked down into his face. She didn't like the bluish tint to his skin. She pressed her palm against his forehead. No fever. She breathed a sigh of relief.

"My ribs are not as sore," he said, attempting a grin. "That's a blessing."

"A big one." She smiled, patting his shoulder. "You lie still while I go whip up the biscuits."

He shook his head. "Don't have any appetite this morning. But I need my coffee."

"You'll have it in a jiffy."

She hurried back to the kitchen, more grateful than ever that she'd bought coffee. There was no point in telling him that Luke had hightailed it. For now, she'd let him think Luke was checking out the back forty.

She grabbed the battered tin pot and reached for the water bucket. She was angrier than ever at Luke—they had saved his life, and yet he had deserted them just when he was needed most.

nine

It was early morning and Luke sat up with his back propped against an aspen tree. He closed his eyes, trying to tell himself he'd done the only thing he could do.

Just before daybreak, he had crept through the darkness to the stable, his bedroll and saddlebags clutched under his right arm. A pale gray light had begun to form on the horizon, and his steps had quickened. Hank would be getting up soon, making coffee. Luke would miss their conversations on the front porch.

He came upon Smoky in the small corral, and his spirits lifted. The big stallion was his best friend; they'd been through hell and high water together. He still counted it a blessing that the no-good thief and backshooter hadn't stolen Smoky. *A blessing*—he was beginning to sound like Suzanne.

He stepped inside the shed to retrieve Smoky's saddle and bridle. The big horse threw his head up and nickered. When Luke lifted the saddle onto Smoky's back, its weight brought a slight twinge of pain to Luke's sore shoulder. The Waters had done a first-class job of patching him up; the wound was quickly healing.

He started to cinch up the girths, and almost before he realized it, he was thinking of Suzanne again. She was good with horses; she sat one like she'd been born there.

What would she think when she awoke and found him gone? Would she care? He tried to tell himself that she and her pa would be disappointed that they'd lost a free

65

hand, but those thoughts brought him shame now. His conscience jabbed at him, and the God he had run from had laid a message on his soul: the Waters were true Christians, setting an example of the way people should live. If all people had treated him as they had, he wouldn't have forsaken his faith. Maybe he hadn't forsaken it, after all.

He left the gate open as he entered the corral. Smoky was already pawing the ground. Luke planted a boot in the stirrup and pulled himself into the saddle, surprised not to feel more pain.

He kept a tight rein, walking the stallion slowly out of the corral. Once they reached the back meadow, he gave the big horse his head, and they tore across the valley toward the lowest knoll on Morning Mountain. Once there, he drew rein and shifted in the saddle. Far behind him, he could see the weathered little cabin outlined in gray light, nestled peacefully in the valley. There had been a few times, at that cabin, when he had experienced the kind of peace and contentment he had been seeking for a very long time.

He had known that kind of life once, but it seemed so long ago and far away that he scarcely remembered how he'd felt. He *did* recognize a longing for that kind of life; perhaps it was the reason he felt so restless and unhappy now. Perhaps it was what drove him, harder and harder, to find something worthwhile again.

Last night, hearing the words Suzanne had spoken in the kitchen, knowing for the first time how destitute they were, he couldn't take another bite of food from their table. It would be like taking food out of their mouths!

Lowering his hat over his forehead and shifting his weight in the saddle, he turned his eyes toward the road ahead. A soft ache settled around his heart, but he'd get over it...

The sound of a prairie dog scampering around the next tree awoke him. He stretched, being careful with his left shoulder, and came slowly to his feet.

He squinted at the road leading to the next ranch. Time to go; time to get on with his life.

ten

"I'm feeling better," Hank called from the kitchen table.

Suzanne was in her bedroom, putting on her riding boots.

"I know." She had been relieved to see that the bluish tint had faded from his skin, but he still looked pale. "I'm just going to make a quick trip over to Trails End to see if Doc Browning has some medicine he wants to send."

Hank was opening his mouth to protest as she hurried off, but she threw up her hand. "Don't waste your breath arguing about it. I'm going," she said and was off.

"Don't have any breath to waste," Hank muttered as the front door closed.

❧

The Little River Cattlemen's Association had been meeting at Trails End once a month to discuss cattle prices and markets. The purpose of today's meeting was to cover last minute details of the cattle drive south to Pueblo.

Arthur Parkinson stood on his porch, looking from Arthur, Junior, lounged against a post, to the ranchers gathered. There was Ben Graves, Harry Stockard, John Grayson and now a tall, dark-haired stranger who had just ridden up, seeking work.

"What did you say your name was?" he asked.

"Luke Thomason." He looked Parkinson straight in the eye and spoke calmly. "I've been on cattle drives in Kansas. I know what has to be done."

Parkinson turned and looked at the other men who nodded their approval.

"All right," he said, "you're hired. We'll be leaving tomorrow. In the meantime, you can put your gear in the bunkhouse and head to the cattle pens to help the hands."

"Thank you, sir." At that, Luke turned and left.

Arthur stared after him momentarily, noting the way he held his left arm close to his side. Still, he looked strong enough. He'd probably do as well as the others, maybe better.

"Here comes Doc Browning," one of the ranchers spoke up. "He's the last one to vote on the price we're accepting for the cattle. Now maybe we can finally get this thing settled and be on our way."

A white horse cantered up the driveway, and the men began to wave.

Nathaniel Browning was a native of St. Louis, attending medical school there, yet choosing the wide open spaces of Colorado to practice medicine. He was a short, rotund man with a giant heart and a penchant for raising cattle.

He had just arrived at the gathering and greeted the other ranchers when once again attention was diverted to another rider loping up the drive.

"It's Miss Waters," Art said, coming to life for the first time all day.

He bounded down the steps and waited at the hitching rail as Suzanne reined Nellie in. She accepted Art's hand as she tumbled from the horse, smiled briefly at him, then made a dash for the front porch.

"Miss Waters, what brings you over?" Art called to her.

"My father." She headed straight for Doc Browning. "Please, come over and take a look at him."

Doc Browning patted her shoulder. "Relax, young lady. Mattie told me about his fall, but he's too stubborn not to mend." He turned to the other men. "Have you men got all the details in order?"

"Just need your vote on the price."

"You have it," he waved a hand dismissively. "Anything else?"

"We're short a cook. Ned's come down sick. Of course Rosa is still going," Arthur stated with a frown.

One of the ranchers groaned. "Without Ned there to keep the chili peppers out of everything, we'll be holding our stomachs."

"Why doesn't someone persuade Mattie to go along?" Doc suggested. "Mattie's a fine cook."

"Who'd keep the post open?" Parkinson frowned.

Suzanne had only half listened to the conversation until now, but suddenly her attention was riveted to the subject at hand.

"I can cook," she offered, looking from one man to the other. "How much are you paying?" She knew she could work out the details if she could have an opportunity to earn some money for the ranch.

Art was at her side instantly. "Oh, no, Miss Waters, you wouldn't want to consider anything like that."

The men turned startled faces to the pert young woman dressed like a cowhand, but looking quite feminine with flowing blond hair and fair skin.

"It'd be too hard on you, Suzanne," The older Parkinson cut the idea short. "We'll find someone. Doc, Mrs. Parkinson is overseeing a big lunch. Why don't you check on Hank and then come back and eat fried chicken?"

"Good idea," he nodded, rubbing his paunch. The subject of food was always of interest to him. "Let's go, young lady."

❧

Doc Browning took his time placing his stethoscope back in his black bag, zipping the bag, then turning to Hank, lounged on the couch. Suzanne hurried in from the kitchen, bearing a tray. Doc rubbed his stomach, remembering he'd missed breakfast. He reached for the mug of coffee and began to munch the fluffy hot biscuit.

"Young lady, this may be the best biscuit I ever put in my mouth," he said, around a generous bite. "But don't tell Mrs. Browning," he winked.

Hank looked disinterestedly at the biscuits then fixed a keen eye on the doctor. "Did I crack another rib?"

Hank was dressed in fresh clothes with his gray hair whisked back from his face, his beard neat. Suzanne had been relieved not to have to tangle with him about his appearance; in fact, he had been quietly cooperative when she'd informed him the doctor was coming. And this, too, worried Suzanne, knowing it was highly out of character for Hank. She wondered if he were depressed over Luke leaving. He'd had very little to say since she had broken that news.

"Your ribs will heal," Doc answered, "and your ankle's doing okay. That's not what has me worried."

Fear clutched Suzanne's heart. "What's wrong with him?"

Doc finished the biscuit and reached for his coffee. He seemed to be stalling for time as he gathered his thoughts. "I'd like Hank to see a doctor in Colorado Springs," he finally replied. "I'm afraid there might be a problem with his heart."

"His heart?" Suzanne repeated, dropping into the nearest chair.

"Aw, Doc, there's nothing wrong with my heart. My chest is just sore from the fall I took."

The doctor appraised him gravely. "Hank, your heart's beating too fast."

"It's cause I got all worked up yesterday," Hank said in a rush, glancing at Suzanne.

"Too fast?" Suzanne echoed. She had resorted to repeating everything the doctor said, but she couldn't seem to form her own words around the fear that was growing in her heart.

"Maybe it'll correct itself in a day or two," the doctor offered hopefully. "Maybe not." He sipped his coffee, staring at the floor for a few seconds. "I read in my medical journal about a new medicine that slows the heartbeat. And I know a special doctor in Colorado Springs who treats patients with heart conditions."

Suzanne took a deep breath, trying to rally her voice since Hank had suddenly gone speechless.

"Well, of course we'll go to Colorado Springs," she said, hardly hearing her words above the fierce pounding of her heart. "We can—"

"I'm not going anywhere!" Hank protested. "If the old ticker's going out, there's nothing they can do. I lost a friend in Denver that way. It'd just be a waste of time and money. . ." his voice trailed, as he avoided Suzanne's face.

She stared at her father. Money, that was what was keeping him from seeing a doctor. Her father was a reasonable man, despite his gruffness. When Doc Browning thought his condition was serious enough to go to Colorado Springs, her father would be willing. It was that nearly empty cookie tin that brought this protest.

"Hank, your heartbeat is strong," Doc continued smoothly, "and you're in pretty good physical condition, considering how rough you treat yourself. That medicine may be all you need to get straightened out."

"What medicine?" Suzanne asked, seizing the hope Doc offered.

"The name wouldn't mean anything to you, but I hear it helps folks. Tell you what," he said, coming to his feet. "I have a colleague who'll be coming in from St. Louis in a day or two. I'll bring him out for a look at Hank. If he agrees with me, I'm going to insist you two go to Colorado

Springs."

Silence settled over the room, broken only by the creak of a floorboard as Doc headed for the door.

"We'll think about this," Suzanne said, reaching for the bundle of biscuits and placing them in Doc's hands. He looked from the muslin-wrapped gift back to Suzanne and smiled, understanding this was his payment for seeing Hank.

"You take care," he called to Hank, as Suzanne walked him out the door. She followed him to the hitching rail, where his white horse pawed restlessly.

"Doc, I need your help," she blurted.

Her outburst startled him. He was about to place a boot in the stirrup, but now he hesitated, looking at the young woman whose gray eyes were fixed worriedly on his face. "What can I do?" Doc asked earnestly.

"There's no money left for this medicine or a trip to Colorado Springs. If I can persuade Pa to go over and stay in one of Mattie's cabins, I want to go on that cattle drive and help Rosa cook."

He began to shake his head. "It would be too rough—"

"Doc," she cried, "who do you think runs this ranch now? And nothing could be rougher on me than watching Pa lie in there sick and helpless, knowing we can't afford the medicine he needs."

Doc lifted a hand to stroke his chin. "It's a good idea about him staying at Mattie's place. If he got worse, she could get word to me a lot quicker than if you two were over here by yourselves."

Suzanne nodded, already making plans. "I can pay Mattie back for her trouble."

"Mattie's got a heart of gold," Doc said, turning his eyes from Suzanne back to the cabin. Maybe it wasn't such a bad idea. Still, there had to be an easier way. "Young lady, don't you two have family up in Denver? Surely, there's somebody to help you."

She shook her head sadly. "No, there's no one. Ma's parents died years ago, and Pa was an orphan. There's only an uncle, and he's the one who cheated us." She bit her lip, fighting tears. "I have to do something, Doc. I'm the only one who can. Please put in a word for me with the ranchers. I can cook for them, you know I can."

He sighed. "Well, if the rest of your cooking matches these biscuits, those men'll be glad to have you along. And Rosa would be there...," he mulled the words over, obviously contemplating the prospect of Suzanne on a cattle drive.

"Doc, will you talk the ranchers into letting me come along? Please!"

She hated begging, but she would swallow her pride and do anything to help her father. He was all she had.

"Who'll take care of your horses?"

"Did I hear you say it was only a two day trip?"

He nodded, stroking his chin. "Pedro owes me a favor. He's a bit slow but honest and dependable. He's been laid up at my place. Maybe I'll send him over here to see to things while you and Hank are away. We're talking four days at the most."

Suzanne grabbed his sleeve. "Doc, if you'll help me with this, I'll never forget it. God bless you!" She leaned up to plant a kiss on his cheek.

Doc Browning grinned down at the pretty young woman, who was about as desperate for help as anyone he'd encountered. How could he refuse? "All right, missy. But you don't know what you're letting yourself in for." He smiled tenderly. "Guess it wouldn't matter. You're about as stubborn as Hank!"

eleven

It had taken both Mattie and Suzanne pleading, arguing, then resorting to threats, before Hank finally realized he was outnumbered and overpowered and gave in. Suzanne suspected it was Mattie's promise of lively conversation with cowboys and stage hands that had finally won him over.

Now as she stood in the kitchen at Trails End, helping Rosa box up supplies, she felt a sense of relief. . .and adventure. She'd been stuck at the ranch for so long, she'd forgotten how excited she could get over a trip, even though this one was a bit different.

She grabbed a box and headed out the back door to the chuck wagon, humming softly. Just as she rounded a corner of the house, she almost collided with a tall cowboy with blazing blue eyes. She gasped, losing hold of the box. She would have spilled everything there in the dust, if he hadn't reached out to recover the tilting box.

"What are you doing here?" Luke stormed at her.

All the frustration that had been gathering since his departure erupted from her lips. "That's none of your business. Anyone who would run out in the middle of the night, without so much as a good-bye—" she broke off, realizing that she was betraying her emotions. She took a firm grip on the box and sidestepped him.

"Wait a minute," he caught up, grabbing her arm. "I didn't run out. I left a note. Besides, I told you I would be leaving."

"Miss Waters!" Art Parkinson's voice echoed from the opposite side of the yard. He was waving frantically.

She acknowledged him with a nod, smiling blankly.

Luke took a step closer, lowering his voice. "I couldn't take advantage of your hospitality any longer. I needed money. When you mentioned cowhands were being hired for this drive—"

"You're going too?" she gasped then tried to steady her voice. "Well, what you do is your business. You can pick up your wedding ring when we return." Her eyes sliced over his face. "I've never needed money badly enough to sell someone's wedding ring. But then," she added bitingly, "perhaps I have more respect for wedding vows than you do."

His dark brows shot up; then his blue eyes clamped into a scowl. She sensed she had gone too far, and now that she had vented her temper, her nerve was deserting her.

"If you'll step aside," she spoke calmly, "I have to get this to the wagon."

A bewildered look settled over Luke's features. "Did you take a job here?" he asked, falling in step beside her.

"I'm going on the cattle drive. I'll be helping Rosa cook."

His mouth fell open. "You can't be serious."

Again, Suzanne was struggling to keep her temper in tow. "Of course I'm serious! And from now on, I'd appreciate it if you'd do your job and let me do mine." She slid the box into the wagon while he stared at her. "Excuse me," she said, sidestepping him as she turned back up the path to the kitchen.

She was practically running by the time she reached the kitchen door. *Luke Thomason! Of all times and places!*

It occurred to her that she had never been so rude to anyone in her life, but she couldn't worry about that now, and she couldn't think about him. She had a job to do.

Rosa stood at the kitchen sink, scrubbing an iron kettle. She was a large Latin woman with warm brown eyes, an abundance of black hair, and a friendly, toothless smile.

Suzanne took a deep breath and smiled at Rosa. "Rosa, what's to go in the wagon next?" she asked, staring at the kettle while seeing Luke's blazing blue eyes.

a

Arthur Parkinson stood at the wagon, staring up at Rosa and Suzanne. Rosa gripped the reins with confidence, her ample body planted firmly on the wooden seat, one booted foot resting on the brake. Beneath her wide hat, Rosa smiled at Mr. Parkinson, assuring him they were ready.

So why does he look so worried, Suzanne pondered as he lingered, glancing once more at Suzanne. She felt a stab of guilt, knowing Mr. Parkinson didn't want her along. It had been the badgering of Doc, and probably Art, Jr., that had forced him to give in.

He drew a breath and began to explain the hazards of their trip: dust, the threat of bad weather, even the possibility of rustlers along the way. He reminded the ladies they were solely in charge of the food wagon, preparing the meals and cleaning up afterward. With over a thousand head of cattle, the men had all they could do to keep the temperamental cattle watered, grazed, and moving in the right direction. They couldn't be worrying about the womenfolk.

Suzanne listened politely, watching the lines deepen in Mr. Parkinson's face as he detailed the problems. When finally he wound down, Suzanne gave him a reassuring smile.

"We'll do our part," she promised, remembering the generous salary they had agreed upon. It would be enough to get her and Hank to Colorado Springs for a doctor and medicine. "And don't concern yourself with me. I'll be just fine," she added.

Mr. Parkinson stared at her for a moment, looking unconvinced. Then he turned his attention to the wagon, checking over the supplies. Suzanne shifted on the seat and peered back into the wagon bed, literally a kitchen on wheels; tools, ropes, and a water barrel were attached to the outside. She couldn't imagine one more item being crammed aboard.

"See you up the trail," he concluded, climbing on his big horse, wheeling around, and cantering back to his men.

As Rosa clucked to the team, Suzanne clutched the edge of the seat and the wagon rocked from side to side, moving them out ahead of the herd. They were supposed to get a head start to insure arrival at the camp site in time to set up for the meal.

As the wagon swung past the cowboys lined up at the corral waiting to herd the cattle, Suzanne spotted Luke in the rear. He was wearing leather chaps, spurs, and range clothes. His blue eyes watched from the narrow space between the low brim of his hat and the bandanna he was pulling over the lower half of his face.

She glanced at the other cowboys. They, too, had covered their faces to ward off the dust they would be eating along the trail.

"Be careful, Miss Waters," Art called to her. He had just arrived, tugging on a hat that looked too wide for his head.

"I will," she called, turning her attention to the road.

Everyone had a bandanna, she noticed, even Rosa. She took a deep breath, wondering why she hadn't thought of it. Well, she would manage, she vowed, watching the brown dust swirl up around the wagon wheels.

They stopped just past noon for a quick lunch while the cattle grazed and drank from a stream. She passed out the egg sandwiches that she and Rosa had packed, along with apples and tea cakes.

The cowboys had seemed self-conscious around her at first, but now they were eyeing her more boldly when Mr. Parkinson's back was turned. Art was clearly irritated by their impudence, and he glared at one, then the other, as he strode through the group to catch up with Suzanne.

"Miss Waters!"

Suzanne turned.

Art's long gangly legs ate up the distance between them. "I thought you might need this." He proudly extended a clean bandanna.

"Why, Art, how thoughtful of you."

"I was afraid you wouldn't think of that," he said with a laugh, setting his Adam's apple in motion.

"Thank you. . . ," her voice trailed as Luke stood before her, his hand outstretched for his lunch.

His blue eyes held a look of irritation, as if he was angry with her again. But then she saw that his eyes were sliding toward Art who was jauntily walking back to his horse.

She dropped the wrapped sandwich into his broad palm, her hand accidentally brushings his. She felt a nervous jolt. Averting her eyes, she moved on, distributing the remaining lunches.

She scarcely had time to gulp down her own sandwich before Rosa motioned for her to help repack the wagon. Suzanne quickly complied, and soon they were back on the trail again.

Far in the distance behind them came the herd, spreading across the plains like a giant brown wave, kicking up clods of dust that seemed to float forward, reaching Rosa and Suzanne. She glanced down at her clothes and saw that they were now rumpled and layered with dust.

Suzanne glanced again at the enormous herd that bawled and bellowed and kicked up enough dust to fill a canyon. She realized at once that she'd taken on an even greater challenge than trying to run the ranch while her father was laid up. But lunch had been a snap; she would eat dust for two days, if that's what it took. She was thankful that Rosa was her companion now, for the woman kept up a lively conversation as she guided the horses. Her words were a mix of Spanish and English, and at times, Suzanne had to guess at what she meant. Still, she enjoyed hearing stories of Mexico City, Rosa's home town.

By mid-afternoon, even Rosa was too weary to talk, and they lapsed into silence as each woman fixed gritty eyes on the horizon.

A shout grew closer and Suzanne leaned out to peer around the back of the wagon. Mr. Parkinson was waving his hat in a circle around his head. She tapped Rosa on the shoulder and motioned for her to look back.

"Stopping for the night," Rosa interpreted, pointing to a grassy valley just ahead.

After their wagon had clattered to a halt in the pasture, Suzanne hopped down, then almost fell flat on her face. She had been sitting for so long that her legs were cramped and stiff; she could hardly walk.

She removed her hat and scratched the crown of her damp head while she squinted back toward the approaching herd. The riders had fanned out, giving the cattle more room as they moved into the far end of the valley. Her eyes scanned the group of cowboys until she spotted Luke, who was intent on keeping the yearlings in line and discouraging strays. He was holding his left arm close to his chest. She wondered if his shoulder was hurting. Well, she couldn't be worrying about him. She had her pa to think about.

Suzanne wandered to the nearest shade tree and dropped down, pressing her weary back against its trunk. They had left Morning Mountain far behind, and she found herself missing that special place that seemed to anchor her at all times. It was a comforting presence to her; as Pa said, it was a place to rest weary eyes and hearts.

Rosa waddled over and sank down in the grass, stretching her large body into a full recline. Suzanne bit her lip, trying not to laugh. She probably had the right idea, Suzanne decided, wishing she had the courage to plop down like that and think nothing of it. Then, as she spotted Mr. Parkinson cantering up, she was glad that she was seated properly against the tree.

"You ladies can rest a bit. We'll need to get water for ourselves and the herd." He looked at Rosa. "Can we eat in an hour?"

Her wide hat bobbed a nod.

"Miss Waters, you see where the stream is, don't you? Over there where the cottonwoods form a line." He said, pointing to the trees. "Help yourself to a fresh drink."

"Thank you," she murmured, dragging herself to her feet. She was even more thirsty than tired, if that were possible, for she and Rosa had drained the canteen two hours earlier.

She stumbled through the thick meadow grass to the line of trees where a stream wound down the valley like a silver thread. She tossed her hat down and stretched out on the bank, lowering her hands into the chattering stream. She cupped her hands to scoop up the cool water, bringing it quickly to her parched lips. She slurped the water greedily, relishing its chill on her tongue.

❧

Luke was aching from head to toe, but the ache in his body and the grit on his tongue did not compare to the mounting frustration he suffered watching the gangly Parkinson kid make a fool of himself. He was still wet behind the ears and about as subtle as a bull.

Surely Suzanne wasn't serious about him. But if she wasn't why was she so friendly with him? Why did she smile and flirt?

He dragged down from Smoky, trying not to grimace from the throbbing pain in his shoulder. Nobody had guessed he was injured, much less lying unconscious and close to death, only a week ago. Somehow he couldn't bring himself to ask Suzanne to keep it quiet. But he had a hunch she would anyway.

Thinking of his own health brought his worries back to what he had heard about Hank Waters on the long dusty stretch of road from Trails End. A twinge of guilt hit him and he began to walk toward the chuck wagon, parked farther up in the meadow. This was free time; most of the guys were doing as they pleased. There was no reason he couldn't have a word with Suzanne. Only there was no such thing as just a *word* with her. Each conversation seemed to end up in an argument.

He knew most of the time it was his fault. He had a bad attitude, but he was trying to change. He frowned. When had he started trying? Soon after he'd met Suzanne. He realized *why* as he spotted her walking toward the trees. Her blond hair glinted in the afternoon sunlight, and from the way she was hobbling across the meadow, he guessed she was as tired as he. Yet, she was the bravest woman he had ever known—except perhaps his mother. In many ways, Suzanne reminded him of her. Perhaps sometime he'd get around to telling her that, and he'd tell her exactly why.

☙

Suzanne drank her fill and lay exhausted for a moment. Something moved beside her, prompting her to roll her head in the grass and look up. She saw a pair of dusty black boots. Slowly, ever so slowly, her eyes traveled from the pointed toes of the boots, up the leather chaps and silver belt—she noted the silver buckle; it appeared to be a rodeo trophy—and on to the collarless cotton shirt. Luke

Thomason stood over her. He had removed the bandanna, along with his hat, and now his thick hair was damp and curling on the ends. Suzanne stared at his head, thinking most women would envy that kind of hair.

"How's the water?" he asked.

"Wonderful." She scrambled for her hat and was trying to work her stiff muscles into standing when his gloved hand touched her arm.

"Wait just a minute, please."

She stiffened, wondering what he was going to say. Well, she was in no hurry, and besides she had been feeling pretty guilty for bawling him out so badly back at the ranch.

She turned and scanned the lush meadow, now a beehive of activity with bawling cattle, irritable shouts from weary cowboys, and the unpleasant smells associated with the beasts.

"Don't worry, I'm not going to say anything about your . . .injury. I doubt that you told them the condition your shoulder was in."

She watched his eyes drop and she knew her guess had been right.

"It's up to you if you want to abuse your body," she said. "I have enough to worry about without being a gossip or worrying about you."

"I came to speak with you about your father," he said, looking back at her.

At those words, and the gentle manner in which he spoke them, Suzanne relaxed her tense shoulders and looked away. Turning back, she stared into Luke's blue eyes as he dropped down beside her, puzzled by his change of attitude.

"Mr. Parkinson told us you had come on this drive to earn money for your father—that he needed to see a doctor in Colorado Springs about his heart. He never mentioned a heart condition to me."

Suzanne's eyes dropped to her hands, nervously bunching the meadow grass. "We just found out the morning you left. Doc Browning came and checked him over. He said Pa's heart was beating too fast."

"If I had known. . . ," his voice trailed as he stared at the western sun, a red ball of fire on the horizon.

"I guess there was nothing you could do," Suzanne replied. "It's just that I had grown to depend on you and I had no right to do that." She hesitated then added, "I'm sorry I spoke sharply to you this morning."

"You did have a right," he said, looking thoughtful. "You saved my life. I figure you're entitled to something in return."

She tilted her head to search his face. "You've repaid the debt by helping out for a few days. And you delivered the colt! We were getting spoiled by you; that's why we hated for you to leave." Her expression changed from sadness to concern. "How's your shoulder?"

"I'm fine." His chest rose and fell as he took a deep breath and slowly released it.

His eyes drifted slowly over her face, and Suzanne felt her heart skip a beat. What did he really think of her? What was he thinking now? She liked him, even more than she wished to admit to herself. She just didn't know what to *do* about it.

"After I rode off, I felt guilty," he said. "I should have said good-bye properly, but. . . ."

"You tried to make amends by leaving the ring."

"Suuu-zannne," Rosa's strong voice belted across to her, and Suzanne dragged herself upright.

"I have to get supper," she said, turning to go. Then she forced her aching muscles into a stiff run back to the chuck wagon.

Luke stared after her, ashamed of himself. He had been

all wrong about their motives in helping him. It was obvious now that they hadn't been trying to trap him or force him to stay. She was still being nice to him; she was still concerned about his health. And she hadn't told on him, like some women would have done if they had felt jilted. Jilted? Why had he thought of that word? There was no courtship between them. But then. . .he would never jilt a woman like Suzanne. He only wished circumstances were different, he wished. . . .

He tore his mind away from such foolish thoughts and turned to get a drink of water.

❧

Suzanne realized, guiltily, that Rosa had already heaved the chuck box from the rear of the wagon and was opening the hinged lid. Cubbyholes and drawers held cutlery, plates, and other staples. From the depths of the box, Rosa removed coffee beans and a grinder.

"I'll get the water," Suzanne offered, grabbing the enormous coffeepot.

Soon they were busily preparing the evening meal. She and Rosa had decided on bacon, beans, and biscuits, topped off with Rosa's fried apple pies. Somewhere in the background, one of the cowboys was playing a harmonica. The jaunty tune he played flowed over the camp, and slowly the cowboys relaxed after their hard day's work, smiles returning to their wind-whipped faces.

Suzanne's eyes trailed from the group back to the skillet of bacon she was frying; she loved to watch the meat sizzle, breathe the unique aroma. She lifted her eyes again, this time to the cottonwood trees where a breeze rippled the leaves. The breeze grew stronger, stretching across the valley—a cooling relief from the heat of the day.

The man playing the harmonica had launched into a lively version of "Oh! Susanna", and a tall cowboy was belting out the chorus while the others tapped their feet, clapped, and stole glances at her.

Even Luke was watching her with a rare grin.

She looked away, embarrassed, but suddenly was very glad that she had come.

Later, as the men sat around the fire, sampling her biscuits and murmuring their approval, Suzanne stole a glance at Luke. He was watching her, she was sure of it. Yet, when she looked at him, his blue eyes skittered over her head, as though he were observing something in the distance.

Daylight gave way to darkness and the men sat around in groups, drinking coffee, discussing the next day's plans.

"Are you doing all right, Miss Waters?" Art asked, slinking up from the darkness.

She gasped and whirled, pressing her hand to her bosom. "You startled me," she exclaimed.

"I'm real sorry," he said, looking distressed.
"That's okay, Art. I'm just a bit jumpy. And I'm doing just fine. Thank you for asking."

He stood with his head tilted, staring down into her face, his arms dangling awkwardly at his sides. As Suzanne looked at him, she realized that any hope of caring for Art had vanished since she'd met Luke. The thought startled her—she and Luke had never even spoken romantically. But she knew that she couldn't settle for anything less than true love, and Art couldn't draw that from her with any amount of attention.

"Excuse me, I need to ask Rosa something," she said, smiled briefly, then sidestepped him.

She didn't want Mr. Parkinson upset with her for distracting his son. Furthermore, she was in no mood to keep up a polite charade with Art. He was beginning to wear on her nerves. For some reason, whenever Art came around, she found herself stealing a glance at Luke, trying to gauge his reaction. He didn't seem to notice Art's attention to her. Or if he did, he certainly didn't appear to care.

Everyone took turns being watchman, so the cattle were never left unattended. Suzanne's eyes followed Luke when his turn came to mount his horse and ride the perimeter. His profile was a silhouette in the darkness, but she could see that he still favored his left side, leaning forward in the saddle, working the horse's reins with his right hand.

"Miss Waters?"

Mr. Parkinson stood over her.

"Yes, sir?"

"You and Rosa throw your bedrolls here beside the chuck wagon," he said wearily. "You'll have more privacy. I'll see that you're not disturbed."

"We'll be fine," she replied quickly.

She believed he considered her to be one more responsibility added to his load. Hating to cause him more concern, she was determined to be as helpful as possible.

After she and Rosa had cleaned up and put everything back in the chuck box, she settled down with her bedroll. From the depths of her pants pocket, she retrieved a tiny square of folded paper. She shook the dust from the paper, frowning, as she gently opened it, careful not to tear the sheet.

The verses she had copied were dim in the light of the lantern mounted on the wagon, but she knew them by heart anyway. Her eyes slipped down the list, pausing on the last one.

"I can do all things through Christ which strengtheneth me."

She thought of this cattle drive, of Luke, and finally of Pa. *God, please make him well,* she silently prayed. Then she folded the paper and nestled down in her sleeping bag, too weary to pray more.

twelve

Suzanne felt a weight on her shoulder, pressing down, pressing harder. Someone was shaking her. Her eyes, gritty from trail dust, dragged open. Rosa's toothless smile greeted her.

She popped up on her elbow, looking around. Some of the men were already up, moving about the herd, checking the horses. She bolted from her bed and fumbled for her boots. Rosa began to motion her toward the back of the wagon. There waited a pan of water and a clean towel.

"Thanks, Rosa, you're a dear!" Suzanne smiled at her.

Suzanne turned and began splashing water onto her face. Her skin tingled from the coolness of the water, and slowly her brain began to clear. She found her mirror, whisked her hair back into a braid, then joined Rosa at the fire.

Although she had spent the night sleeping on the ground, she felt surprisingly well. She fell quickly to the task of mixing biscuits, then relieving Rosa at the big frying pan where slabs of bacon sizzled. The smell drifted over the cool spring morning, and Suzanne quietly prayed for a good day.

After breakfast, Mr. Parkinson came up, taking the chuck box from Suzanne's hands and fitting it into the wagon for her.

"You ladies, hurry up," he said. "With luck, we'll make it into Pueblo by dark." He held himself erect, squaring his shoulders as though preparing to go to battle.

Pueblo served as a crossroads for travelers flooding into

Colorado. It also provided a railhead for shipping cattle. It was a bawdy, dusty settlement nestled in a wide valley, looking rather plain to Suzanne compared to her hometown of Denver. But Suzanne and all the others on the cattle drive considered it paradise after another day beneath a blazing, merciless sun.

During lunch break tempers started flaring among the cowboys. Luke looked out of sorts. Even Art seemed rather sullen. Rosa, usually cheerful and pleasant, had lapsed into silence until the dust-layered chuck wagon lumbered into the outskirts of Pueblo. Then she blew a huge sigh and turned to give Suzanne a wide smile.

"Mr. Parkinson said to look for the Antlers Hotel," Suzanne instructed her. "That's where we'll be staying tonight."

Both women squinted into the setting sun as the wagon clattered down the narrow main street. A couple of general stores, two banks, a livery, and a narrow, two-story hotel were scattered about with a number of saloons sandwiched in between. Music drifted through the saloon's swinging doors, as women in colorful dresses beckoned cowboys inside.

Suzanne turned on the seat and glanced around the town.

"That's the only hotel I see." Suzanne pointed to the building on the corner. Trail dust gritted against her teeth as she spoke. "Yes, there's the sign, Antlers Hotel!"

Rosa carefully guided the wagon onto the side street that paralleled the hotel and stomped a boot to the brake. Suzanne leaned back in the seat, wondering if she could possibly walk after another day of sitting on the hard wagon seat.

They were just getting their feet planted solidly on the ground when Mr. Parkinson rode up.

"I'm going in to pay for your rooms," he called to them. "The others can fend for themselves. Art and I will be staying here too, if you need anything." His eyes lingered on Suzanne.

"We'll be fine." She smiled back, wishing he would stop worrying about her.

"In the morning, Johnny, my best cowhand, will escort you back to the ranch. The rest of us will be staying on to sell the cattle and take care of business."

"Thank you, Mr. Parkinson," Suzanne called after him, but he was already around the side of the building. "He's always in a hurry, isn't he?" she commented to Rosa.

As the women entered the hotel, Suzanne could tell from the shocked stares of those in the lobby that she and Rosa looked a mess. The desk clerk took a step backward as she and Rosa approached the counter, and he shoved the registration form across for their signatures. They must smell like cattle too!

"You do it," Rosa handed her form to Suzanne, who signed for her.

"Second floor, last room on the right," the desk clerk quickly instructed, handing each of them a key. "Will you be wanting a tub of water? It comes with the room."

"That would be wonderful," Suzanne replied.

They hurried up the steps, trying to ignore the shocked faces of two proper women, on the arms of their husbands. On the second floor, Suzanne found her room and pointed Rosa toward hers. She unlocked the door and stepped into a small yet nicely decorated room with polished mahogany furniture. A marble-topped night stand held a kerosene lamp beside a lush bed. She stared at the bed for a moment, taking a deep long breath. She couldn't wait to hop in!

Then her eyes fell to her dusty boots. Out of respect for the carpet, she reached down and removed her boots, careful not to add any more dust to the mounting pile. Depositing her overnight bag, she slipped off her woolen socks and sauntered to the window to raise the shade.

Below her, the busy street was filled with horses, wagons, and an assortment of people. She recognized two cowboys from the cattle drive. They were pushing through the bat wing doors of a saloon across the street. She pressed her face against the window, peering right to left. Where was Luke, she wondered. Probably in the saloon already. She lowered the shade and sighed. She had hoped he wouldn't forget the lesson he had learned from his last poker game.

The knock on the door turned out to be her tub, carried by two stout men who eyed her curiously. Suzanne didn't notice their stares, as her eyes drifted longingly to the tub. The men then brought up pails of hot water. As soon as they left, she forgot about Luke, the long trail, and everything else for the next glorious hour as she soaked in the tub.

When finally Suzanne felt squeaky clean and presentable in a floral cotton she had tucked into her satchel, she left her room. She knocked on Rosa's door, planning to invite the older woman to dinner, but from the sound of the snores audible through the wooden door, Rosa had forgotten food.

Suzanne ventured cautiously down the stairs, wondering what Mr. Parkinson expected them to do about supper. She had brought the last dollar from the cookie tin, hoping it would be enough to cover her expenses until Mr. Parkinson paid her.

As she stepped into the crowded lobby and glanced

around, she heard her name shouted above the murmur of voices.

Art Parkinson came, fresh from a bath and shave, dressed smartly in a top coat over black trousers. From the looks of the crisp white shirt, she suspected his first stop in town had been the general store.

"I was on my way to your room to see if I could buy you supper," he said, beaming at her.

Suzanne hesitated. Automatically, her eyes slipped over the lobby. Luke was nowhere in sight.

"The dining room is filling up fast," he continued, "but we can still get a seat."

She smiled up into Art's angular face. She should be grateful someone wanted to escort her to the dining room.

"That's very sweet of you," she said, taking his arm.

She dragged her eyes from the lobby of strangers and walked with Art into the dining room, unaware that Luke was just entering the hotel. And now he was watching her walk away with Art.

Luke entered the opposite side of the dining room, carefully selecting a table in a far corner. He sat in back of Suzanne so he could observe her without her knowing it.

Taking a deep breath, he studied the menu that had been handed to him. He had been starved when he had arrived at the hotel, half hoping to invite Suzanne to eat with him. Mr. Parkinson had given them a slight advance to see them to Pueblo, and he hadn't spent any of it. There was enough to buy dinner for two this evening.

How could he have forgotten about Junior, he wondered, glaring in their direction.

The young idiot hadn't stopped talking since they'd sat down. He squinted, trying to see how Suzanne was reacting, although it was hard to tell, with her back to him.

And yet she was tilting her head, nodding, acting like what he was saying was the most fascinating speech she'd ever heard.

"Ready to order?"

The waiter stood by his table, waiting.

Luke looked back at the menu. Well, he had enough money for two, so he'd eat enough for two.

"I'll take the beef steak, potatoes, whatever else comes with it."

"Thank you, sir."

The menu was whisked from his hand. Immediately, his eyes shot back to the couple. Then, with firm resolve, he turned in his seat and concentrated on looking through the window to the busy street. He would not look their way again, he promised himself. It was a matter of pride, and he knew he could be tough enough to keep that promise.

ðŸ‚·

Suzanne had listened intently as Art had give a lengthy account of his year at Harvard. He had managed to talk his way through their delicious meal. Suzanne began to wonder if all this talking was a nervous habit or if he was this loose jawed all the time. "I would have flunked out if not for Papa pulling a few strings," he stated proudly. "One year was more than enough for me. I was born to be a rancher," he boasted.

She listened and forced a smile. From what she had observed, Art spent more time lounging on the porch than at the corral and stables. She supposed when your father owned the ranch, other things mattered—like wearing good clothes and supervising the ranch hands.

Maybe life with Art wouldn't be so bad, she told herself, recalling the satiny feel of the fine hotel soap, not the rough lye she'd had to rub on her skin for months.

". . .And I would be honored," he finished with a flourish.

Her eyes moved from his bobbing Adam's apple to his flushed face. He had obviously said something very important, but she had no idea what it had been.

"So. . .how do you feel about that, Miss Waters?" He was such a gentleman, always addressing her formally.

"Well. . .," she hesitated, wondering how to react so he wouldn't know she hadn't been listening.

"I guess I'm speaking prematurely," he rushed on. "I know you have to see to your father, but, like I said, next year when I turn twenty-one, I'd like to ask for your hand."

She gulped, wondering how she could have possibly missed his proposal. She mentally scurried to recapture her wits, knowing the importance of choosing precisely the right words.

"Art—and please call me Suzanne from now on—you understand how worried I am now, with Pa and all."

"Oh, yes! I hope you don't think I'm being improper."

"No, not at all! I appreciate everything you've said, and I'm honored that you—" she broke off, swallowing. "I just think we should wait a while longer to discuss this. But, thank you." She gave him her best smile.

He was staring into her gray eyes, transfixed, blithely unaware that his size-twelve feet blocked the passage of the drunken cowboy stumbling past.

Suddenly, a crash just behind her jolted Suzanne, and she whirled to see a huge man sprawled across the adjoining table. A goblet shattered against a china plate; silver clattered to the floor.

Sputtering profanities, the man gathered his considerable bulk upright and whirled on Art, spitting fire. "You tripped me!" he roared, slamming a huge hand around Art's throat.

Suzanne stared at the hammy hand, crushing Art's Adam's apple. *Why, he could choke in seconds,* Suzanne thought and panicked.

"I. . .didn't. . ." Art choked out the words between gulps for air.

"Turn him loose," Suzanne cried. "You fell over your own feet, not his."

The man turned raging eyes to her. His companion had now joined the ruckus, snickering in the background. Suzanne glanced at Art whose bulging eyes could pop from his face any minute.

"Well, you're a feisty one," his companion said. "I'll see to her, Buster."

The proprietor rushed up, desperate to settle the matter quietly.

"Step aside," the bully growled at him. "Me and this idiot will settle our differences outside." He yanked Art from the chair and hauled him from the dining room.

"Come on," the companion breathed whiskey into her face. "We don't want to miss the fun." He was every bit the bully his friend was, Suzanne decided, as his fingers bit into her arm.

"Stop this," she cried, looking back at the proprietor who was trying to quiet the disrupted diners, assuring them everything was under control. There had merely been a small disagreement.

Didn't anyone care? Couldn't anyone stop these bullies?

Suddenly the ugly man who had grabbed Suzanne was shoved back and knocked flat. Luke stood over him, glaring down threateningly.

"Leave the lady alone," he warned through clenched teeth.

Suzanne gasped, looking from the man to Luke, then back again. Suddenly, she remembered Luke's sore shoulder, and the desperation she had felt for Art was nothing compared to the concern that rushed through her now.

The man was scrambling to his feet, his fists balled, when a commotion in the front of the lobby brought a dead silence to the group.

The sheriff and two of his deputies stood with guns drawn. "Buster, you and your no good partner saddle up and ride out of town," he ordered. "Otherwise, you'll spend the night in jail. I warned you, there'd be no more fights!"

The big bully loosened his hold on Art, and now Art's long legs buckled and he crumpled to the floor, gasping for breath.

"Your boyfriend needs you," Luke drawled.

"He's not my boyfriend," she hissed under her breath.

"Then you have no right leading him on the way you do."

She threw her head back, staring into Luke's face with flaming cheeks and flashing eyes. "How dare you speak to me that way!" she sputtered, forgetting that he had come to her rescue. She suddenly seethed with anger toward Luke. *How could he be so stupid?* Then she saw Art sprawled out on the floor, clutching his throat. She ran over to kneel down beside him.

"Are you all right?" she asked, smoothing Art's rumpled coat.

He was still gasping for breath, but at the sight of Suzanne leaning over him—her face flushed with concern—a bruised smile touched his purple face. He leaned against her, luxuriating in the comfort of her arms.

The crowd had begun to disperse. When Suzanne ventured a glance over her shoulder, Luke was gone.

"Uh oh," Art muttered, and Suzanne followed his worried eyes to the direction of the stairs. His father was charging toward them, his eyes boiling with anger.

"Here are your wages," he snapped at Suzanne, shoving a wad of bills into her hand. "You and Rosa be ready to leave first thing in the morning. And Art," he whirled on his son, "you and I have business to take care of."

Art didn't utter a sound as his father waved toward the front door, and the two marched out without a backward glance.

Suzanne had stared after them, thinking that was how it would be if she were ever foolish enough to marry Art, whose father barked out the orders and Art snapped into place.

Embarrassed and close to tears, she hurried to her room, yanked off her clothes and jumped in bed. Taut with nerves, her aching body lay rigid on the feather mattress for several minutes. Then, stretching her sore limbs, she told herself to forget the disaster downstairs and enjoy a comfortable bed, a luxurious room. The crisp sheets caressed her skin, and a pillow of softness cradled her head.

Still, she could not sleep.

She judged it to be midnight when finally she crept across to the window, sneaked the shade up, and peered down at the sidewalk.

Cowboys still milled about in twos and threes, talking and laughing. She didn't recognize any of the men from the ranch, and she wondered where everyone had gone. Her eyes settled on the swinging doors of the saloon across the street. She squinted down, trying to make out a familiar form in the blur of people. It was hopeless. In the smoky haze of the saloon, it would be impossible to recognize anyone.

Was Luke in there, she wondered, creeping back to bed. She closed her eyes. In her memory, she saw the look of scorn on his face, heard his scalding reproach. What troubled her even more, however, was her own behavior. She had rushed to Art's side, merely to spite Luke. She had wanted to hurt Luke—she had tried. Tears of shame filled her eyes. What had gotten into her?

Art shouldn't have let the man bully him that way, one side of her brain argued. Why, she had shown more nerve than Art. At least she had stood up to the men, while Art had done nothing to defend either of them.

How could he, when he was being choked? the other voice argued. Luke would have defended himself and her. He had come to her side even though she had been with another man. He'd been ready to fight for her, and would have, even with an injured shoulder.

She stared at the plastered ceiling, wondering exactly how Luke felt about her. As much as she wanted to believe he cared for her, she could find nothing of substance on which to pin her hopes. He probably would have come to any woman's defense. He was, after all, a gentleman, even though he could be gruff and argumentative. *Like Pa.* Was that one reason she was drawn to him?

Tears trickled down her cheeks in the darkness as the strain of the past week took its toll. Her mind jumped from concern for Pa to concern for Luke. And finally, she had one more thing to worry her. For days she'd tried to explain away her reaction to Luke. Tonight the truth had caught up with her.

I'm falling in love with him, she thought miserably, *and I might as well admit it.* It seemed hopeless, for Luke was obviously still broken-hearted over his wife; maybe he would never love another woman the way he had loved. . .G. Suzanne didn't even know her name.

She saw in her memory the wedding band with the two hearts linked together. She cried harder.

"Lord, touch his heart, please. . .and heal the broken places," she prayed.

thirteen

Luke left the hotel lobby abruptly and stood outside, breathing deeply of the night air, trying to calm his temper. He was almost as angry with Suzanne as he was with the Parkinson kid.

She would end up marrying him and living a miserable life. If money and security were that important to her, then she could have both with his blessings.

No, not his blessings.

He stared across the street to the rowdy crowd entering and leaving the saloon. He was too tired for that, and now his shoulder was killing him.

"Thomason!"

He turned to see Mr. Parkinson charging toward him, fumbling with a wad of bills. The son cowed at his side, looking thoroughly subdued.

"We can settle our own matters," the older Parkinson said tightly. "You don't need to trouble yourself."

Luke stiffened. The man was obviously mad at his son but taking it out on everyone else. He'd seen that before.

Parkinson was peeling off bills from the wad in his hand. "Here's the wages we agreed on. You're free to go."

Luke nodded, accepting the money. "Thank you, sir." He spoke with respect to the older man, but as he turned to walk away, his blue eyes slid to Art and narrowed, as his lip curled in contempt. Then, he turned and made his way to the livery.

Suzanne's return home had been uneventful. Johnny, an older cowhand with red hair and freckles, had arrived at the hotel just after daybreak to escort them. Suzanne suspected that Mr. Parkinson was trying to get her out of town as soon as possible, before she caused more trouble! Johnny had taken over the team, freeing Rosa and Suzanne to take turns napping in the bed of the wagon. They had made camp that night, then reached Trails End by the next afternoon.

Hurriedly, she had fetched Nellie and ridden away from Trails End. She was grateful for the money and relieved that she and Hank could go to Colorado Springs, but she feared she had alienated the Parkinsons.

As she topped the knoll and the log outpost came into view, she felt like bursting into tears. She hadn't realized how tense she had become the past four days. Now, seeing familiar territory brought a feeling of enormous relief. Everything looked peaceful. Only a few horses were tied at the hitching rail in front of the store.

Her eyes scanned the cabins out back of the post as she wondered about her Pa. She hoped he hadn't been too grumpy with Mattie, who had kindly offered to wait on him.

She clucked to Nellie who seemed to recognize the familiar territory as well, for she quickly responded, and they galloped across the valley in record time. Suzanne slowed Nellie up as they reached the front of the log building, then hopped off, looping the reins over the rail. She hurried toward the front door, ready to make excuses for Hank's behavior. When she pushed the door open and entered, she saw Hank reclining at the table in the rear, a coffee mug between his hands, a wide smile creasing his thin face.

Mattie stood in the kitchen door, listening intently as Hank entertained two cowboys with a tale of his rodeoing days.

As the door slammed behind Suzanne, all eyes flew to the front of the room.

"Suzanne!" Hank roared, grinning from ear to ear. "You made it back." The grin disappeared as he looked her up and down. "How did that cattle drive turn out? Did those fellows treat you all right?"

"Everything went just fine. Rosa and I tended to our business, they tended to theirs. We got to Pueblo, spent the night in a wonderful hotel, then Johnny drove Rosa and me back."

Hank scratched his chin. "Everything turned out okay, huh?"

"Just fine. How've you been?" It wasn't a lie, she told herself, she had just told her Pa what he needed to hear. She leaned down to give him a big hug, forgetting the soreness in her body.

"I'm getting fat and sassy from Mattie's cooking!"

Suzanne turned to Mattie, who was coming forward to greet her, arms extended.

"I'm mighty glad to see you," Mattie said, squeezing her hand. "He's been worried and frankly so have I." Her brown eyes made a sweeping inspection of Suzanne. "You've lost a few pounds."

"I'll find them soon enough. Has he given you any trouble?" Suzanne asked, dreading to hear the answer.

"No. He's behaved himself just fine," Mattie smiled.

Suzanne saw the tenderness that touched Mattie's features as she looked at Hank. Was there something different in Hank's eyes, as well, Suzanne wondered, as he grinned at Mattie.

"I've had some mighty good meals," he said, patting his stomach.

"Doc Browning brought a doctor from St. Louis," Mattie informed Suzanne. "He agrees your father should see the doctor in Colorado Springs."

Hank fell silent, staring at the floor.

Mattie put an arm around Suzanne's shoulder. "Bet you could use some beef stew."

Suspecting Mattie might have something more to tell her, she nodded with enthusiasm. "That sounds wonderful."

Once she and Mattie had reached the privacy of the kitchen, Mattie's smile faded. The brown eyes she turned to Suzanne now held a look of concern.

"He hasn't complained, but I see him touch his chest several times a day. I'm worried."

Upon seeing her father, Suzanne had felt as though the invisible burden that weighed her down had suddenly been lifted. Now, that weight returned, crushing her again.

"I can take him to Colorado Springs." She glanced toward the dining room. "We'll leave tomorrow, if possible."

Mattie was staring into the dining room, deep in thought. "I don't think he should ride a horse," she whispered.

Suzanne sank into a chair, bewildered.

"Mattie, I hadn't even thought about that. How could I be so dumb?"

Mattie hugged her. "Child, there's not a dumb bone in your body. We just forget Hank's not up to doing the usual."

Suzanne nodded sadly, hearing her father's voice merrily relating another rodeo story.

"I asked him about the wagon you brought here," Mattie continued. "He said it's still in the barn. Could you take it? That way he could stretch out in the bed if he gets tired."

Suzannne looked back at Mattie, suddenly wondering

how they had managed without her.

"That's a wonderful idea."

"I'm sure you could get one of those cowboys to go along," she inclined her head toward the dining room. "You could give them a wage."

Suzanne pursed her lips, thinking it over. She hated the idea of paying someone when she and Hank might need every dollar. "Let me think about that."

"I know your pa will say he doesn't need any help," Mattie said. "And maybe you two *can* make it on your own. Wish Lilly was here so I could go." She shook her head, looking frustrated. "Listen, I have a dear friend who runs a boardinghouse there. The least I can do is let her know you're coming. She'll take good care of you."

Suzanne turned back to the woman who had become their best friend. "How can I thank you for all you've done for us?"

Mattie's eyes had strayed to Hank. "Just bring him back healthy, and that'll be thanks enough."

ॐ

Luke stared into the campfire, trying to sort through the confused thoughts muddling his brain. As soon as Parkinson had paid him off, he had stalked to the livery, resaddled Smoky, and ridden out of Pueblo. He'd wanted to put distance between himself and everyone else, particularly Suzanne.

He had ridden for a couple of hours, letting the cool darkness wash over him, calming his frustration and anger. He had made camp late, sealed in cozy darkness with only the sounds of Smoky munching grass and a squirrel playing in the tree.

As the campfire dwindled, he found himself thinking back to his mother and the good principles she had instilled in him. His conscience was tugging at him, telling him that Hank Waters needed him. The man had been like a father to him, and he didn't know when he had enjoyed another man's company as much as he had enjoyed being with Mr. Waters.

He'd heard Johnny complaining about having to get up early and drive the women and the chuck wagon back. Apparently, Junior was staying in town with Daddy.

Luke frowned.

Did Suzanne plan to take Mr. Waters into Colorado Springs with no help?

He stood, kicked out the campfire, and reached for his bedroll. He'd sleep on it. Since he was going to Colorado Springs anyway, he just might offer to help.

❧

Suzanne walked through the house, relieved to be home. She kept recalling the way Mattie had looked at her pa. Was Mattie thinking of her father as more than a friend? He had mentioned Mattie several times, as well. *They might just be a good match for each other,* Suzanne thought as she sat on her bed, yanking her boots from her weary feet. Instead of feeling a surge of joy over the idea, she was disappointed in herself to experience a twinge of jealousy.

How could she deny her father happiness in his old age? Well, knowing her father, nobody would deny him anything if he made up his mind. She stretched out on her narrow bed, then turned on her side, snuggling into the pillow.

"It's not meant for man to be alone," her mother had often told her. That was true. It would be good for her father to have a companion in his old age.

What about me? she thought wearily, wondering where Luke was by now. Halfway to Colorado Springs, no doubt.

She was almost asleep when the distant sound of hoof-beats penetrated her semiconsciousness. Her lashes parted, her eyes drifting open. Was it Pedro coming back? He had left soon after they had arrived. He'd taken good care of the horses. She had asked him to stay on while they were in Colorado Springs, but first he wanted to return to Doc's ranch for the night.

The hoofbeats were real and coming closer. She sat up in bed, wondering if Mattie had sent a cowhand to check on them.

"Suzanne," her father called, tapping softly on her bed-room door.

"Come in," she called.

He opened the door and looked at her with puzzled eyes. "Luke's riding up," he said.

fourteen

She couldn't have been more surprised. She had thrown on a housedress, brushed the tangles from her thick hair, then taken an extra moment to compose her thoughts.

Hank's voice flowed throughout the cabin, offering coffee, answering Luke's questions about his health. Suzanne took a deep breath and opened the door.

Luke sat with her father at the kitchen table, sipping the brew, munching on one of the tea cakes Rosa had packed for them. They were discussing her father's heart condition. At the sound of her steps, Luke turned in the chair and looked across the room.

Their eyes met and Suzanne caught her breath.

He needed a shave, his blue eyes looked weary and haggard, and his clothes held a layer of trail dust. Yet, she had never been so glad to see anyone in her entire life.

"Hello," she said, smiling at him.

"Hello," he nodded, preparing to stand.

"Keep your seat. Please." She sauntered across the living room to stand at the end of the table. "You must be tired."

He nodded. "What about you?"

Suddenly, *she* didn't feel tired at all. She felt as though she could run all the way to the trading post.

"I've rested." She wandered back to the coffee pot, pouring a small amount into her mug. She really had no taste for coffee at this hour, but she needed to occupy herself in some way, and maybe she needed a reason to join them at

the kitchen table. Her eyes surveyed Luke's dark hair—
thick, waving at his neck and around his ears.

"Did you get home all right?" he asked in a casual tone,
glancing at her.

"Yes, Johnny drove us back. Rosa and me," she added,
then wondered why she felt compelled to explain who had
accompanied them. "He insisted we get an early start."

Hank cleared his throat. "She tells me there were no problems on the drive. I'm mighty proud of her."

Suzanne's eyes flew to meet Luke's face. His expression
was inscrutable. She knew the man well enough to know
he would not mention the ugly scene at the hotel if she
didn't want him to. For once, she was glad he was close-
mouthed. This was not something she wanted Hank to hear
about.

"Your daughter did remarkably well under the circumstances," he said, studying the tea cake.

Under the circumstances! She cleared her throat, settling into a kitchen chair. "I assumed you were halfway to
Colorado Springs by now. Or already there."

He was studying his mug, taking his time to answer.
Just why had he come here, she wondered wildly, although
she wasn't about to ask. She was just glad that he had.

"I've come to help you and your father get to Colorado
Springs. If you want me to, that is."

That announcement seemed to startle Hank as much as
Suzanne. "Well, that's mighty decent of you," Hank said,
shifting his thin frame against the wooden chair. "We sure
could use some help."

Her father's statement was equally surprising. It was
totally out of character for Hank to accept help. Allowing
Mattie to fuss over him was one thing; admitting that he
couldn't manage a team of horses or get himself to

Colorado Springs was quite another.

"I thought we'd get the wagon out of the barn, make a bed in the back," she said, glancing worriedly at her father. She hadn't even broached the subject with her father, dreading his reaction. Now the words spilled forth unchecked, and she hesitated, waiting for another objection. Hank drank his coffee in silence.

Luke looked at Hank. "What about a team? You wouldn't want to use your good horses."

Hank had the answer. "Reckon we could pay Parkinson to use some of his work horses. He's got plenty." Hank's blue eyes drifted to Suzanne. "Since you're so friendly with them, maybe you could ride over and ask in the morning."

Suzanne's eyes shot to Luke, silently pleading.

"I'll do that," he offered. "I'm sure your daughter will have plenty to do here, preparing for the trip. When did you want to leave?"

"Tomorrow," Hank said on a deep sigh.

Suzanne stared at her father. He obviously felt worse than he had admitted, and this scared her. But with Luke sitting here in the kitchen, making plans to help them, the invisible weight on her shoulders had magically been lifted again.

Hank retired to his bedroom early, claiming to be tired. Suzanne could see he was too excited about the trip to be sleepy, but she appreciated his attempt to give them privacy.

Luke sat in the kitchen chair, staring at his empty mug, saying nothing.

"Want some more coffee?"

"No, thank you." He glanced at her.

"Tea cakes?"

"Nothing else."

He kept looking at her as though he wanted to say something. *What? The ring!* He wanted the ring back! And he was willing to see them to Colorado Springs since he was headed there anyway.

"Excuse me for a minute," she said.

She got up from her chair and went to her bedroom. She opened the drawer and withdrew the letter, recalling briefly the disappointment she had felt upon reading it.

The wedding band fell into her palm, its soft burnished gold gleaming in the lantern light. Gripping the ring tightly, she returned to the kitchen and placed it on the table before him.

"You came for this," she said.

His eyes dropped to the ring, then shot to her face. He leaned back in the chair, and she watched the grim expression he so often wore slip back over his features.

"You think I came here just to get the ring?"

She swallowed, nervously wondering if she had sounded abrupt or unkind.

"I know what it means to you," she stammered.

"How do you know that?" he asked quietly.

"Well. . . ." Her eyes fell to the gold band lying in the center of the table, so small, yet suddenly seeming to outweigh everything in the room. Even her words lay heavy against her tongue. "I assumed. . . ," she faltered again.

"You have a bad habit of doing that," he drawled.

She stared at him. "Doing what?"

"Assuming things."

"But the inscription on the inside," she blurted, "the hearts. . .G. . .L—" she broke off, her cheeks flaming. Her eyes flew to a darkened corner of the room. He must think she was the nosiest person he'd ever met. She'd had no right to. . . .

"That ring doesn't belong to me," his voice cut through her puzzled thoughts.

Slowly, her eyes drifted back to him as she tried to absorb his words. *What did he just say? The ring doesn't belong to him?*

"Then who. . .why?"

His suntanned hand shot out, plucking up the simple band that had created such furor. He held it to the light, reading the inscription almost as though he had forgotten about it.

Suzanne stared at the ring, confused. Had he simply found it on the trail? What about the L? Was it possible he was lying to her?

"The ring belonged to my mother," he said at last. "Her name was Grace. The L is for Luke."

Suzanne sank into the chair and planted her elbows on the kitchen table.

"Luke is your father?" she asked, leaning forward, searching his face.

He nodded, saying nothing more as he casually dropped the ring into his shirt pocket. "My mother died recently."

She swallowed hard. "I'm sorry. And your father?"

"Is in Colorado Springs."

"Oh," the word fell from her throat. "You two are starting a new life there, like Pa and I have?"

A bitter laugh sliced the air, startling Suzanne. "No. Not the two of us. He started a life there long ago, when he deserted Ma and me. I'm taking the ring because she begged me to, so I could prove I was his son. Otherwise, I doubt he'd recognize me."

Suzanne's mouth fell open as her mind scrambled to take this in and provide the right response. She looked from Luke to the ring.

"You might as well know the truth," he said flatly. "I made a promise to my mother on her deathbed. I'm merely keeping that promise. Then I'll be going back to Kansas."

She stared, her mind jumbled with questions she knew better than to ask. He had already shared something very private, something that had obviously broken his heart as a young boy. She sat silent, unable to speak. Luke stood, pushing the chair back under the table.

"I can sleep in the barn," he said.

"No, you'll sleep on the couch." She got up and went to fetch a blanket and pillow. She returned, placing both on the couch. "Good night," she smiled, then turned and headed to her room.

Going back to Kansas. . . Going back to Kansas. . . The words bounced through her brain for the next hour as she tossed and turned on her bed, and the sleep she desperately needed eluded her.

❧

Their old prairie schooner was still in remarkably good shape, after being uncovered from the back of the barn and cleaned up for the trip to Colorado Springs. Suzanne had spent the morning organizing the items they would need. There had been a few tears shed in private when she'd touched the wooden box she had found on a shelf in the barn—the box they had used to pack supplies for their trip down from Denver. Suzanne recalled her mother choosing and packing the cooking utensils in this box, chatting excitedly with Suzanne about their new home. She still missed her mother desperately, but Suzanne knew she was in a better place.

The sound of Luke's horse brought her back to the task at hand. She walked out of the barn and waited for him to reign Smoky in and report the outcome of his trip to the

Parkinson ranch.

"I've arranged for a team."

"Wonderful." She began to stroke Smoky's gleaming neck.

"Johnny is bringing the horses over in an hour," he continued. "We'll allow a day, even two if necessary. That will give us plenty of time to stop and rest. I can trail my horse behind the wagon."

Suzanne nodded, reaching into her pocket for the last lump of sugar. "Sorry you have to trail the wagon," she said, tucking the lump into the stallion's mouth.

She looked back at Luke. "Thank you for taking care of things," Suzanne said. "We really appreciate what you're doing. Did they mention what they're charging us for the team?"

She had vowed to be as agreeable as possible, and now both were acting as though the conversation in the kitchen had never taken place.

Suzanne tried not to think about the Parkinsons, and didn't even ask whom Luke had spoken with about the team.

"I'll pay them whatever is fair," she said.

He removed a package from his saddlebags, mumbled something about "already paid" and hurried toward the house.

❧

Now, she sat on the wagon seat beside Luke while Hank stretched comfortably on quilts and pillows in the bed of the wagon. She had begun to suspect that her father was working some secret plan, for he had become suspiciously docile. He had allowed them to wait on him and do all the planning, while he'd merely nodded agreeably to whatever had been suggested.

Suzanne recalled what Mattie had said—that he had a habit of touching his chest at intervals. She noticed this as well and suspected it was an unconscious effort to still his rapid heartbeat. Yet, he had not complained; he even seemed excited about the trip.

The metal fasteners jingled against the leather harness as the horses plodded dutifully up the road to Colorado Springs. She had prayed for good weather, and God had obliged them with a gorgeous spring day, complete with a light breeze and enough clouds to offset the sun.

Luke had left the canvas flaps open so Hank could talk freely with them from the back of the wagon, but the old man had said little. She glanced back and saw that he was dozing. Behind the wagon, Luke's horse sauntered along, looking as though he resented being hitched to the wagon.

She stole a glance at Luke. He was wearing fresh pants and a black shirt, which looked suspiciously like one she had admired at Mattie's store. She wondered how much money he had earned on the cattle drive. Clearing her throat, she forced out the words that had been nagging her since his arrival, "I want to apologize for seeming so. . . ungrateful the other night in Pueblo."

Beneath the black felt hat, his blue eyes narrowed on the road ahead.

"I'm sorry I was rude," he replied.

"You weren't," she answered slowly. "You were trying to help, and I appreciate that."

He turned and looked at her, and Suzanne saw an expression of tenderness in his eyes.

"You remind me of my mother," he said.

"I do? Tell me about her."

"She was pleasant and sweet, like you. She tried to see the best in people."

Suzanne blushed at the compliment. "And you think I'm like her? I don't know about that!"

He grinned. "You have a temper, but as far as I can tell, that's your worst trait. You're kind and forgiving, like Ma," he added.

"Did she forgive your father for leaving?"

A muscle clenched in his jaw, and Suzanne wished desperately that she hadn't asked. She didn't want to evoke unpleasant memories or turn the conversation in the wrong direction. But it was too late now, the words had already been spoken. He was opening his mouth, looking at her. He might tell her to mind her own business.

"I couldn't understand," he said quietly, "how she could keep on loving him, but she did. She said I look just like him; I probably act like him too. I remember him being a pretty stubborn critter."

"How old were you when he left?" she asked as gently as possible.

"Twelve. My parents had worked hard, scrimping and saving to move to Colorado. They were going to homestead here. He left with the money, promising to return when he had found the right piece of property. That was the last time we saw him."

She caught her breath. "Surely there was an explanation?"

"Yep. He met another woman."

Suzanne stared at him, wishing he would elaborate, but he sank into gloomy silence. She turned her eyes toward Morning Mountain in the distance, which usually gave her a boost of courage. "My mother shared Pa's dream, as your mother did," she said, glancing at Luke. "I suppose that's natural for a woman."

His eyes slipped back to her, searching her face. She

wondered what he was thinking.

"It was strange," Suzanne continued. "Ma couldn't even stay mad at her brother—despite his deception. She thought this was a beautiful place to start a new life, doing what Pa wanted to do."

"Surely your pa was less forgiving."

"Pa was mad, all right. But we were here, and it *is* a beautiful place. Maybe it was meant for us to start over. Ma read the Bible a lot, gave us verses for comfort. We might gripe about my uncle's trickery sometimes, who wouldn't? But we've managed to survive without being bitter."

"That's hard to believe," he said flatly.

"Tell me," she faced him, "do we seem like bitter people to you?"

He turned and looked at her; then he began to shake his head.

"No, you don't. You and your pa are the nicest people I've ever met." He turned back to the road, breathing a sigh. "I could never be that forgiving. Ma and I nearly starved. She scrubbed floors and washed dishes for people in the daytime and took in ironing in the evenings. I looked older than my years so I lied about my age to get men's work."

"Surely things got better for the two of you?"

He nodded. "I worked my way into a foreman's job at a big ranch out from Abilene. The owner, Mr. Godfrey, was in bad health, and the foreman before me had done a poor job. There were financial problems. Mr. Godfrey promised me if I'd run the ranch like it was mine, he'd pay me well. I was willing to work for less pay if he'd deed me some land. My family had never been able to own land of their own—it was always our dream."

He stopped talking, taking a tighter grip on the reins.

"You can't stop the story now," Suzanne said, touching his sleeve.

"I broke my back for two years, taking little pay, dreaming of the day I'd own my own section of land. Then his daughter decided she wanted to marry me." He shook his head slowly. "I couldn't muster up any feeling for her, and I didn't want to spend my life with a woman I couldn't love."

"I can understand that," Suzanne replied. She could scarcely believe that he was confiding such personal matters.

"I reckon you can," he grinned. "You've got the same situation with young Parkinson."

Suzanne looked down at her fingers gripped tightly in her lap. How could he guess what she was going through? It must've been written all over her on the stock drive. "I won't marry him either," she said.

"You won't? How do you know you wouldn't be happy with that rich family?" he asked.

"Because I don't love him. He isn't the type of man I'd want to spend my life with."

He was looking at her carefully. "And just what type of man do you want?"

"A man who's strong yet tender, who enjoys the things I enjoy. A man I truly love."

They were staring deeply into each other's eyes. Suddenly the wheel struck a large rock, sending them bouncing. The impact jarred the wagon, and something clattered in the back. Suzanne heard a yelp of pain from her father.

"What's going on?" Hank shouted.

Luke leaned back in the seat, tugging hard on the reins

to slow the panicked horses.

Suzanne turned, peering through the parted the canvas flaps. "We hit a rock."

Hank was leaning out the back of the wagon, trying to calm Smoky. Glancing back over his shoulder, he beckoned to Suzanne. "I think you best get back here and let me take a turn on the seat," Hank suggested. "Luke may need my help."

The horses had finally settled down to a leisurely pace.

Suzanne swapped places with her father and stretched out on the quilts, enjoying their comfort. Her father had closed the canvas flaps, so she couldn't see the men. Still, she could hear her father's voice.

"Blue Sky people, the Utes were called, and they were the only Indians who were the real natives here. Owned a bunch of magic dogs," Hank chuckled. "Know what magic dogs are?"

"Horses, I'd guess," Luke replied.

"Horses they got from the Spanish." Hank sighed. "Reckon they had a pretty good life here in the shadow of the Peak until all us greedy white folk arrived. . . ."

As Hank's words droned on, Suzanne closed her eyes, knowing she needed the sleep. But she couldn't stop thinking about what Luke had told her, and the fact that he *had* told her such personal matters. She smiled to herself. Maybe, before this trip was over, she could change his mind about going back to Kansas.

fifteen

Suzanne bent over the campfire, stirring up the stew she had brought along. Luke was rubbed down the horses, while Hank leaned back on a flat rock, smoking his pipe and studying the dying sunset.

"Pretty sight, isn't it?" he asked, his eyes fixed on the raspberry glow settling over the mountaintop.

"It's beautiful," she sighed, glancing at the breathtaking sunset. "Pa, I love it here."

Hank stared at her and suddenly his gray eyes held a sheen of tears. He looked back at the fire. "The older you get," he said slowly, "the more you look like your mother."

Suzanne's eyes flew back to him. She was pleased by his compliment because her mother had been one of the prettiest women she'd ever known. She had inherited her mother's fair skin and blond hair, but she longed for her round face and her beautiful light blue eyes, like the sky in early morning.

"You've told me I sound like her, but I'm not as pretty. I know that."

He glanced at her. "Yes, you are. You're not as delicate perhaps, but God knew what He was doing. You had to be more hardy to survive here."

Suzanne heard him speak those words and, fearing that he was thinking back to that awful blizzard that had led to her mother's death, she rushed to fill the silence.

"Tell me about when you first met her. I love hearing that story." She glanced at Luke to see if he was listening.

He was feeding the horses but was still within ear shot.

"Abigail was about your age when I first spotted her. I had ridden into Denver from the ranch where I was working. My boss's wife needed a bolt of cloth to make clothes for their new baby. 'Just ask Mrs. Ferguson,' I was told."

He shook his head, glancing at the clouds. "I didn't know anything about womens' cloth, and I was scared to death I wouldn't find this Mrs. Ferguson. Sure enough, I didn't. She was sick that day, but her daughter was working in her place."

He looked at Suzanne, and his gray eyes began to twinkle. "Found out her daughter was named Abigail, and she was the prettiest girl I'd ever seen. I was lucky she knew as much about choosing cloth for baby clothes as her mother, maybe more."

"Ma was a wonderful seamstress." Suzanne smiled proudly. "Too bad I have none of her talent."

"Well, she had enough for both of you," he sighed. "The clothes she made for you and her. . . ."

Suzanne leaned forward, wondering if he was thinking about the overloaded wagon they'd brought on their first trip out.

"If you're still worrying about making us throw out the trunk that day—we forgave you. Besides, you warned us we were packing too many dresses. And I know it was either that trunk of extra dresses or our trunk of food that had to go. Ma said she could make us more dresses."

But she never did, Suzanne thought sadly.

Hank shook his head, angrily tapping the ashes from his pipe. "It was the worst thing I ever did. If I hadn't been mad at the team and the weather and that sorry wagon wheel, I'd never have thrown out those trunks to make it on. . . ."

"Pa, you threw out your trunk with the books and rodeo stuff! Will you stop being a martyr? Besides," she leaned back, crossing her arms, "let's just dwell on the good memories. And we have plenty of those."

He looked across the dwindling fire. "I was blessed to have all those years with your mother. I still miss her, but I thank God for you. You've made us both proud."

She stared at him, suddenly at a loss for words. Her father rarely got sentimental. He looked so frail by the firelight. Suzanne wondered if his compliment were somehow an admission of his own failing health—that he might not be around long enough to say the things he really felt.

"Everything's going to be all right," she spoke softly. "I believe that, and you must believe it too."

He nodded. "I know." He stroked his gray beard thoughtfully. "We gotta hold on, keep believing we'll get all these problems worked out."

She reached over and touched his hand. "We will work them out, Pa."

***

They ate quietly. The past week had begun to take its toll on Suzanne. By the time the water was hot for washing dishes, she was nodding off.

Hank and Luke seemed tired as well, and yet the silence that slipped over them was a contented one as the soft darkness sealed them into a cozy circle near the sputtering campfire.

Hank offered Suzanne the wagon bed, saying he'd spent too many nights sleeping under the stars to pass this one up. She didn't argue, and she wearily crawled into the wagon bed and was asleep in minutes.

When she rolled over the next morning and peered at the sunlight seeping through the slats of the wagon, she felt a warm joy spreading through her. Why? She sat up, wondering why she felt so happy on this particular morning.

Then, as if in answer, Luke's voice drifted to her. She heard the pop of the morning campfire and smelled bacon sizzling. Lifting her arms above her head, she stretched lazily. The events of the previous day and evening sifted through her mind, and she smiled to herself. Luke seemed to care for her, and he had been wonderful to Pa. He was exactly what they needed in their lives. If only. . . .

Reaching for her hand mirror, she stared into a pair of shining gray eyes framed by a tousled mass of blond hair. She opened the lid of the trunk, searching for her brush. Underneath the pantaloons, she retrieved the brush and began to rake out the tangles. Once her hair was smooth and gleaming, she decided not to tie it back. She liked the way Luke glanced at her hair. Though he'd never said anything, she had an idea he admired it when she wore it unbound.

She dressed quickly, choosing her blue cotton. Spreading her hands over the skirt, her fingers worked at the wrinkles, trying to smooth them out. After she had done the best she could within the confines of the wagon, she emerged and glanced around.

Pa and Luke sat at the campfire as Luke cooked their breakfast. When Luke spotted her, he nodded politely and inclined his head toward the back of the wagon.

"There's a pan of water on the tailgate of the wagon," Luke said, as his eyes swept over her.

"Thank you," she smiled. "Pa, how do you feel?"

He was perched on the same rock where he had sat the night before, contentedly sipping his coffee.

"Like I could break the wildest mustang in the west!"

Luke grinned at him, and Suzanne merely shook her head

as she made her way to the back of the wagon to splash water onto her face.

Just as they had done the previous evening, she and Pa prepared to say grace before eating. Suzanne noticed that Luke did not bow his head, and this made her uncomfortable. Hank seemed not to notice. Perhaps ignoring him was the best way to handle Luke's strange moods.

Luke ate his food in silence. Suzanne wondered if their prayer had brought on his dark mood. And why, she wondered. She soon gave up trying to start conversation.

After he'd shoved down his meal, Luke hurried to get the team ready to travel. Suzanne met her father's eyes across the campfire.

"Pa, what's wrong with him?" Suzanne asked under her breath.

Hank winked at her. "He's just doing some soul searching. Leave him be."

"I intend to," she snapped, hopping up from the campfire and grabbing the dishes to be washed.

❧

Luke's mood improved once they were on the road and Hank brought up the subject of horses.

"I got a lot of dreams for that little ranch," Hank said. "There's wild horses up that canyon behind our house. The mustang I was chasing. . . ," his voice droned on, and Suzanne's mind wandered. Luke, on the other hand, was mesmerized by the subject of mustangs.

She had given Pa her seat on the wagon and slipped back to tidy up the wagon bed. She knew both she and Luke were facing a challenge once they arrived in Colorado Springs. She and Pa must face the truth about his heart—whatever that was—and Luke would finally confront his father.

A stiffness settled into her shoulders, and she took a deep breath. The next few days could change all of their lives.

She reached into her trunk and pulled out the worn family Bible she had tucked in before leaving. Reverently, she turned the pages, tissue-soft from years of use. She found a comforting chapter in Psalms and began to read. Slowly, the headache that had threatened went away, and she began to relax.

At their lunch break, Suzanna was ready to engage in spirited conversation with her father, while Luke looked as though he needed some time in the bed of the wagon. Occasionally, he rubbed his forehead, as though he might have a headache.

"Wouldn't you like to grab a quick nap?" she asked, giving him a smile as she washed up the dishes.

He shook his head. "I'll catch up on my rest once I get back to Kansas."

The words struck her like a blow, and she turned quickly, scrubbing hard on the eating utensils. What had she hoped for, expected? Whatever it had been, she was obviously dreaming. Luke was determined to go back to Kansas! And why did he keep making a point of it, anyway? Nobody was going to beg him to stay, certainly not her or her pa.

Well, maybe he and his father will patch up their differences, a hopeful voice argued. But what if they did? If he stayed in Colorado Springs, she'd never see him either.

She fought against the depression creeping over her as she packed the cooking utensils beside the first-aid kit in the bed of the wagon. The joy she had felt had been snatched away by Luke's matter-of-fact statement about returning to Kansas.

Hank was putting out the fire when Suzanne came around

the wagon. Their eyes met briefly before she busied herself checking to see that everything was packed. He seemed to sense the tension between her and Luke.

"What if I relieve you driving for a while?" Hank offered as Luke hitched the team to the wagon.

"No, sir. You'd better not strain yourself." He led Smoky around to the back of the wagon to tether him. "But I wouldn't mind hearing more stories about those mustangs," he called back.

That meant Luke wanted her pa to sit on the seat beside him. Well, she could take a hint! She crawled into the bed of the wagon and said nothing more to Luke. If she was not going to be seeing him again, she had to protect herself from any more heartache. The less she had to do with Luke the better off she would be.

She closed her eyes and tried to sleep as they jostled toward their destiny.

❧

Colorado Springs had been founded in 1871 by General William Palmer. General Palmer had envisioned Colorado Springs, situated at the base of Pikes Peak, as a resort where the dry air and high altitude would help those suffering from tuberculosis. He further intended this town to be a cultural center, with an opera house, fine dining establishments, and European-style hotels.

Mattie had told her all about the town, having wintered here with her husband when they'd first come to Colorado. Then they had decided to migrate south to open the trading post.

"Old Man Palmer had no idea, when he designed the town, that the gold rush and the railroad would bring in so many roughnecks!" Mattie had laughed.

Suzanne found herself missing Mattie. If she were along,

she would make them laugh, maybe give her a little advice about how to forget Luke Thomason!

As their wagon clattered down Cascade Avenue, Suzanne stared in awe at the mansions—mostly wood, with a few made of stone. Lace curtains fluttered at the windows, and some of the porches had lovely flower boxes. Someday, she vowed, their ranch house would look like a real home.

She studied the women coming and going. Wearing fancy hats and beautiful dresses, they lolled along the sidewalk, silk parasols in hand, ready to protect their delicate faces if the sun should pop out.

Suzanne shrank back in the wagon, unwilling to be reminded of how little she now owned.

The wagon pulled up before a modest building. Suzanne knew from the conversation between her pa and Luke that this was the office of Dr. Horace Crownover, the physician Doc Browning had arranged for her father to see.

She took a deep breath, forgetting fashion and lovely ladies, and she prayed Dr. Crownover would be able to help Pa.

sixteen

"It could be worse," the doctor said, adjusting his spectacles. He was scarcely five feet tall; still, he was a commanding presence with snapping hazel eyes and a deep, confident voice. His manner was courteous yet reserved, but Suzanne sensed a razor-sharp intelligence.

She and Hank sat opposite the doctor's desk, where he was looking over the notes he had made after examining Hank.

"I'll need to do some more tests before I make any conclusions, Mr. Waters," Dr. Crownover said. "However, I believe the new medication will help you."

Hank had scooted to the edge of his seat, awaiting the doctor's report.

"Do you think I can go on ranching?" He took a deep breath, glancing at Suzanne. "Or is my condition. . . ?"

"With medication, I believe you can go back to a fairly normal life. You may have to alter your activities somewhat."

Hank frowned at that. "What do you mean?"

The doctor hesitated. "Let's wait and see what the medication does. I'd like to start you on it right now. I have a few here," he opened the center drawer of his desk and withdrew a package. "Plan to stay in town for the next few days so we can be sure there are no adverse reactions."

"Yes, we'll be here," Suzanne answered quickly. "We'll be staying in a boardinghouse on Tejon."

126

"Good!" The doctor stood and extended his hand to Hank. "I'd like you to come to the office twice a day."

It was obvious from Hank's sullen expression that this suggestion did not appeal to him; however, he kept silent, allowing Suzanne to make the necessary arrangements.

Luke was waiting for them outside the doctor's office. He had been pacing back and forth on the board sidewalk. When they emerged from the building, he hurried to Suzanne's side, his blue eyes anxious.

"I think this physician will be able to help Pa," she said, smiling. "He's already started him on some medicine."

"I'm mighty relieved to hear that, Mr. Waters."

The men exchanged understanding looks. She wondered if Hank had said more about his heart to Luke than to her. She knew he had tried to be brave about this—that he didn't want to worry her.

"Doc is having a buggy and driver sent over. You coming to the boardinghouse with us?" Hank inquired of Luke. "Mattie telegraphed that friend of hers, and she's expecting us."

Luke shook his head. "No. If you want me to put the team up at the livery, I'll do that. And I reckon we could leave the wagon there too." He turned and scanned the busy street. "I have business of my own to take care of now."

Hank put a hand on Luke's shoulder. "Is there any way we can help you, son?"

Luke shook his head. "No."

"Where will you be staying?" Suzanne asked, trying to sound casual. "In case we need you," she added, looking at Hank.

Luke shrugged. "I'm not sure. The last address I have is from the woman he lived with. I guess I'll start there."

Suzanne touched his arm. "I'll be praying for you."

He yanked his arm away. "Prayers don't help me. They didn't help Ma either. Maybe they work for you people," his eyes blazed from Suzanne to Hank, "but not for me."

Suzanne was too shocked to respond, but Hank said, "We'll see about that, Luke."

Hank's voice had a calming effect, and now Luke dropped his head. "I shouldn't have spoken out in that way. I'm sorry."

❦

Miss Martha's Boardinghouse was a two-story, white, clapboard building with green shutters and a wide front porch. Rocking chairs were assembled about the porch, lending a homey atmosphere to the place.

Luke had unloaded the wagon, then hastily said goodbye. Suzanne stood in the front door, staring after him with sad eyes while Miss Martha yammered on, giving a lengthy account of her friendship with the Wileys.

"Could we get to our rooms, please?" Hank interrupted her, pressing his hand to his chest.

"Oh. Of course!"

Miss Martha was a small, thin woman with white hair and inquisitive blue eyes. She moved with remarkable speed for her sixty years as she lifted her skirts and crossed the foyer to unlock a door on the right.

"I've given you my two front bedrooms, seeing as how you have this weak heart. . . ," she stated.

Hank winced at that but Suzanne linked her arm through his and smiled up at him. "Pa, I just know Dr. Crownover is going to help you. This medicine will work. I'm confident of that."

She *did* feel a confidence in this matter. She just wished now she could stop worrying about Luke.

seventeen

Luke lingered in front of the livery, giving Smoky a lump of sugar. "That's your reward for trailing a wagon for two days. Good boy," he stroked the big stallion's neck.

He glanced up and down the busy street and told himself he had to get on with the task at hand. He swung into the saddle.

Bennett Avenue. The instructions the blacksmith had given him were easy enough to follow, allowing his mind ample opportunity to reflect on the letter Ma had saved all these years—the only letter they'd received from Pa once he'd come here. Luke had jotted the address down on a slip of paper and that was now the address he was seeking.

He turned down Bennett Avenue and glanced around. It appeared to be a respectable area, although the houses were small and close together. He slowed his horse, finding 708.

It was one of the smallest houses on the street, yet the wood looked to be in good condition, and there were lacy curtains at the front windows.

He sat on Smoky, staring at the house. The curtain fluttered; someone was watching him. He got down from the horse, aware that he must look ridiculous, staring at the house like a simpleton. Before he had made his way up the stone walkway, however, the door had opened and a young woman had stepped out, holding a baby in her arms.

"Hello," he said, tipping his hat.

"Hello. Are you looking for someone?"

"Matter of fact, I am." He swallowed, suddenly finding the name difficult to speak. "Luke Thomason."

She frowned. "Who?"

He repeated the name, though he could tell by the woman's expression she had never heard of him.

"We've lived here for five years," she informed him, "but I've never heard that name. Before that, another family named Wilkinson owned the house."

Would his father have changed his name? "Don't suppose Mr. Wilkinson was from Kansas, was he?"

She quickly shook her head. "No, they came here from Tennessee."

He glanced toward the other houses. "Do you think it would be all right if I checked with your neighbors?"

She shrugged. "Sure." Then she turned and went back into the house. He could hear a key locking the door behind him as he turned to leave.

Occupants of the other houses gave him blank stares and shook their heads. Most, he learned, had only lived on the street for the past few years. One woman had offered to check with her elderly father, who was seated in the back yard. Luke had waited outside, nervously twirling his hat between his hands. She had returned, shaking her head, offering no new leads.

"He never heard of him either."

Luke had thanked her and walked back to Smoky. He climbed back in the saddle and left Bennett Avenue. He had done what he could to find the man who'd abandoned them. His eyes drifted upward, as though speaking to someone in the clouds. "I tried," he said quietly.

❧

Luke had found a cheap boardinghouse on the outskirts of town. It occurred to him that he seemed to be trying to get as far from Suzanne as he could. And he knew why.

He'd tried to keep a wall built around his heart, but she had managed to knock that wall down with a gentleness he had not believed possible. For the first time in his life, he was a man in love. He had a better understanding of that emotion now. Real love began with friendship, admiring and respecting that person as he had Suzanne. From the beginning, he had been drawn to the delicate features, the thick blond hair, the shining gray eyes; but soon he had moved past that to learn to know the real woman underneath. Here was a woman a man could easily picture as his wife. She was kind and gentle and patient and caring...and still the prettiest woman he had ever known. Maybe it had something to do with the inner beauty that radiated out of those gray eyes.

He still felt bad for speaking sharply to her about that prayer business. He had reacted before he could stop himself, and now he knew why: she had struck a nerve. That's why he was so touchy. His conscience had started to jab him...like right now. And he didn't want to listen.

He had been lying on a lumpy cot in the small room, staring at the cracked ceiling. Now he hauled himself to his feet, reached for his hat, and headed out into the darkness. He mounted Smoky and began to ride, enjoying the feel of the crisp mountain air on his skin.

Carriages and wagons lined the boulevard leading into town. Colorado Springs was a busy place, growing, thriving. Still, his taste ran toward the quiet countryside, a place like the one where the Waters lived. There a man could feast his eyes on a green valley, the only population being his horses.

But that was their home, not his. He was on the verge of becoming attached to the ranch, as he had to the people.

He had been eager to ride away before he committed himself to something.

When Amanda Godfrey had wanted to marry him, there had been no way he could imagine committing himself to a woman for life. But now, he felt certain he could do that with Suzanne; he even wanted to do that. But he was scared. He had been like his father in so many ways. "Exactly like your father," his mother had often said. Maybe he was afraid there was some dark side of his nature that would keep him from staying with a family. And he would never want to hurt anyone the way he and his ma had been hurt.

He tugged on the reins, slowing Smoky down at the corner. Down a side street, piano music and laughter drifted to him. He saw cowboys entering a saloon, and feeling lonely, he headed in that direction.

He turned Smoky in at the hitching rail and climbed down. Adjusting his hat on his head, he wondered why he'd spent the past hour thinking about Suzanne when he was so dirt poor he had nothing on earth to offer her.

For a while, Hank had become like a father to him, but that wouldn't work either. He probably couldn't live up to the Waters' expectations of him as long as he was wrestling with these demons inside of him.

His boots thudded onto the boardwalk and hesitated before the swinging doors. A cowboy was leaving with one of the saloon girls. Both looked as if they had been at the bar too long. He almost turned away but something drew him inside.

A haze of cigar smoke hung over the saloon as Luke entered the swinging doors, pausing just inside. He was forced to blink and squint, allowing his eyes to adjust to the dim interior after leaving the sunshine outside. The room reeked of liquor and smoke, and he had an urge to bolt.

No, he was going to have a stiff drink. It had been a long time since he'd done that, but he deserved one, didn't he?

"Well, hello there."

Cheap perfume touched his senses before he turned to the young woman in the tight, green satin dress. Luke's eyes swept past the feather in her auburn hair to the uptilted face, heavily rouged.

"Hello," he replied curtly, then looked away.

He could see more clearly now, and his eyes moved past other women mingling with men around the room. Finally, his gaze settled on the mahogany bar on a side wall. He began to walk in that direction.

"That one ain't too friendly, is he?" a male voice spoke from behind him.

"Who cares?" He heard the young woman reply.

He glanced back over his shoulder and saw that she was already approaching another customer entering the saloon.

Luke elbowed up to the crowded bar, staring uninterestedly at the array of bottles and glasses reflected in the wall mirror. A rotund bartender with thick mustache and sideburns worked furiously to fill orders. Luke waited, his eyes scanning the smoky haze, when suddenly he wondered how a place like this had ever held any appeal to him.

He squinted at the woman in the green satin dress, thinking how she, too, had nothing to offer him. Nothing whatsoever.

Then the conversation of the cowhand next to him captured his attention.

"Got a real poker game going in the back room. Big Jake's cleaning out some little fancy pants."

Luke straightened, glancing through the smoke to the door at the rear. He made his way around the tables, his curiosity mounting. He had no interest in another poker game, but the description of "fancy pants" could fit the little scoundrel who'd ambushed him outside of Bordertown.

Cautiously, he entered and looked around. It was a large room with several games in progress. However, it was easy to figure out where the interest was. Several men had gathered around a table in the back. Luke headed in that direction.

Before he reached the table, one of the men left the circle, and through the opening he spotted the little weasel he had met in Bordertown—the one he felt certain had shot him.

His heart pounded as he drew closer. He wasn't sure exactly what he should do, but at the very least, he would confront him. Just then, he heard a gasp spread over the crowd.

The little man had leaped to his feet and pulled a derringer.

"You've cheated me!" he shouted.

Luke was close enough to see that the big cowboy had won all the money, and now the giant came slowly to his feet.

"Now look here," he said. "I won fair and square. Put that gun away."

The little man was out of control. A sheen of perspiration covered his face; his beady eyes were glazed like a drunk's. Luke's eyes dropped to the table. There were no bottles or shot glasses there. He wasn't drunk; he was crazy.

"I'm gonna kill you," he said, wild-eyed. He raised the gun and took a step backwards, knocking his chair over.

The chair banged against the floor, and the crazy man jumped, turning his head toward the noise. In that split second, his opponent whipped out a gun and fired.

Disbelief flickered over the little man's face before he hit the table.

Luke backed against the wall and closed his eyes. He hated to see a man killed, even when that man had invited it. Luke knew if there was ever any hope of recovering his money, his last hope had died with the man. Stunned, he stumbled back to the bar as someone ran for the sheriff.

Above the roar, the bartender's voice reached him. "What'll you have?"

Luke looked from the bartender to the bottles lined up on the counter. He shook his head. "Nothing."

He stalked out of the saloon and stood on the boardwalk, breathing deeply of the fresh air. He had hoped a shot of bourbon would calm his nerves, but now it occurred to him he was looking in the wrong place for strength. He wouldn't find strength in a bottle; he'd have to reach down deep in his soul for that.

He walked stiff-legged toward Smoky. If the hour weren't so late, he would go to visit Suzanne. Saloons and everything within held no appeal to him, probably never would again.

As he walked Smoky from the noisy street, he realized it was not just the poker game, the bullet in his shoulder, and his stolen wallet that had changed him. Meeting Suzanne and Hank Waters had changed him more dramatically than anything else.

For some reason, the verse framed in their house rose up in his memory. *"All things work together for good...."* If he'd not gotten himself shot and ended up in their valley, he never would have met them. What if he had missed knowing her, if only for a short while?

As he reached the quiet outskirts of Colorado Springs, he found himself thinking about another person: his father. What kind of woman had he found here? What kind of life had he lived all these years? And what had happened to him?

❧

He waited until the next day to visit Suzanne and her father, and now his spirits lifted as he spotted them seated on the front porch, rocking, listening to the little woman who stood before them, her lips moving rapidly. He saw the happy expression on Suzanne's face when he halted Smoky and swung down.

"Hello," Hank called to Luke as he approached the front porch.

"Good afternoon." Suzanne was smiling too. He could sense that they had really forgiven him. They weren't holding a grudge about the rude words he had spoken yesterday.

Suzanne got up out of the rocker and came to stand beside him on the porch steps. "Have you found out anything?"

He nodded. "I went to the address. The people who live there never heard of him. Nor had any of the neighbors."

The disappointment was obvious on his face. No matter how hard he tried to pretend he didn't care about finding his father, it mattered more than anything to him now.

She touched his arm. "Don't give up. Someone in this town is bound to have known him."

He shrugged, unconvinced. His eyes moved on to Hank as he climbed the steps.

"Last night I saw the man who robbed me, or rather the man I suspected of robbing me."

Hank bolted out of the rocker, then pressed his chest. "You did? Where? What did you do?"

Luke sighed. "I didn't have a chance to do anything. He was killed after a poker game—accused someone of cheating." He glanced back at Suzanne. "I wasn't in the game."

Luke sank into a rocking chair; Hank followed, still gaping at him.

"That's all there is to tell," he said, looking from Hank to Suzanne. "I didn't find one man, but I found another. Guess I was too late both ways."

Suzanne frowned, following Miss Martha into the house, back to the kitchen.

"What'll you people want for supper this evening?" Miss Martha asked.

Suzanne glanced around the kitchen, her eyes lighting on a platter of chicken left from lunch. The cabbage salad that had gone with it had been tasty as well.

"Would you mind," she asked impulsively, "if I packed some of that chicken for a picnic supper? Luke is feeling low, and he probably hasn't eaten. I think a picnic would perk him up."

Miss Martha beamed. "Great idea. Take him over to the park. It's not far from here. The walk would probably calm your nerves too, young lady. You look a bit over wrought."

She nodded. "Yes, I am."

"I'll entertain your father," Miss Martha offered quickly, smiling to herself as she bounced around the kitchen, gathering up containers. "Just leave it to me," she called over her shoulder, then began humming.

Suzanne sauntered back to the porch, wondering if Luke would like the idea. It occurred to her that her father's nerves were overwrought as well; he could use a walk and a picnic lunch. No, this time she had to think about Luke. Pa would understand.

≥∙

The afternoon sunshine spilled over the small grassy park where couples strolled together and children played.

"Are you hungry?" she asked as they reached a bench and sat down.

"Not just yet."

Across from the park stood a steepled building—a church with white clapboard and stained glass windows. He glanced away, his eyes resting on two elderly gentlemen seated at the next bench.

"Seeing that man who shot you," Suzanne said, " must have been awful."

Luke leaned back, staring up at the sky. "I felt a terrible rage come over me. Then, when I saw him get shot . . . ," he took a deep breath. "Anyway, I just want to forget it. I learned something important last night. I don't ever care to go in a saloon again, and there won't be any more poker games."

The elderly men were getting up to leave. Their conversation drifted into the silence that had fallen between Suzanne and Luke.

"Well, enough about the war. That was a long time ago," one man was saying.

Suzanne cleared her throat. "Was your father in the war?"

"Yes. Apparently, he felt a strong responsibility to serve his country. I don't know what changed him from a loyal soldier to a coward who abandoned his family twelve years later!"

Suzanne caught her breath. It hurt her to hear him speak such bitterness, but she supposed it was good for him to talk about it, much better than keeping all the anger and hurt shoved down deep to fester in his heart. At the same time, she understood his reserve with her. At times he looked at her as though he really cared—he had told her private things about his family. Still, she was never sure when to ask questions or when to keep silent for fear of upsetting him.

"Luke, don't you have any good memories of him?" she asked in a kind, caring voice.

He closed his eyes, passing his hand over his forehead.

"Sure. He taught me how to track a squirrel, how to sit a horse, how to fish the stream down behind our cabin. Those are good memories, and that's why it took me a long time to understand how he could just ride off and never look back."

"When you find him, he may have an explanation for you."

"Oh, he'll have an explanation. The other woman. She even wrote to my mother," he glanced at Suzanne, his eyes glazed with bitterness. "That was after a short note from him. She said Pa was living with her, that they loved each another, but he didn't have the heart to write and tell us. In her letter, she claimed she wanted to tell us so we wouldn't worry that something had happened to him when we never heard from him again."

Suzanne swallowed. "What did your mother do?"

"She wrote back immediately, asking to hear those words from him, rather than her. He never answered. She wrote a couple more times, but we never heard anything."

"Perhaps the letters didn't reach him?"

"They were never returned to us, so he got the letters all right. I guess he just lost his head over the woman." His eyes slipped over Suzanne's features, and he thought about how pretty she was. Since he had met her, he could better understand how a man could lose his head over a woman.

"Luke, what was the woman's name? Do you remember?"

He shook his head. "I don't know what Ma did with the letters, threw them away I guess. I never saw them again. I do remember," he frowned, "it was a name I'd never heard before. Don't guess I've heard it since."

"What kind of name? Try to remember."

He stared into space, his eyes narrowed. "I remember Ma saying something about a flower. The woman had the name of a flower; something unusual..."

"What kind of flower? Rose? No, that's not unusual. A pretty flower? Was it a flower that grew in Kansas?"

He shook his head slowly as his eyes returned to her. "I don't know. It was a long time ago."

She tried to conceal her disappointment. *If only he could remember the woman's name!* It could be more important than his father's name, she believed, if the woman had lived here long enough to make friends. But then, they must have left town, since nobody knew his father.

She tried to suppress a sigh of frustration. There was no point in pressing him. That could only make matters worse for him.

"Well," she said, reaching for the picnic basket, "I don't know about you, but my stomach tells me it's time for supper."

"Good idea," Luke said. "Where do you want to picnic?"

"How about here?" She led the way to a private area beneath a large cottonwood.

"Perfect," he said, sinking down on the grass and removing his hat.

His dark hair tumbled about his forehead, and as his eyes began to soften, Suzanne looked at him, for the first time imagining him as a boy with tousled dark hair and glowing eyes. That would have been before his father had left. She suspected Luke had turned into a man overnight, trying to protect his mother and help put food on the table.

Luke tilted his head, looking at her. "When are you going to open that basket?" he asked teasingly.

"Right now." Suzanne said, turning her mind back to the present. She opened the basket and spread the cloth Miss Martha had thoughtfully included. Then she put out the chicken and cabbage salad, the plates and utensils.

"Oh, no," she looked at Luke. "I forgot the tea."

"Doesn't matter," he smiled at her. "This is a real treat."

They ate heartily. Suzanne thought the chicken tasted even better cold. She was glad Miss Martha had packed plenty of it, for Luke kept reaching for more.

A contented silence flowed between them as they enjoyed the food and the picturesque setting. Suzanne looked up from the church across the way to the dry goods store on the corner, and on to a hardware store down the block.

"This is a nice town," she said, "but I miss our peaceful little valley and our own special mountain."

"Morning Mountain," Luke mused. "That sounds nice. Who gave the mountain that name?"

"Mattie says the first settler into the valley named it. She didn't say why, but I can guess. That mountain is beautiful in the morning. . .looking at it helps to start my day off right."

Her eyes returned to the church and she glanced at Luke. He had followed her gaze there and was solemnly studying the steeple.

"Suzanne," he turned to her, "since we're sitting here in

the shadow of the church, I need to explain something to you."

She was dabbing her lips with a linen napkin. "Go ahead."

"Well—" he broke off, folding his napkin.

"Please, go on. Say whatever you're thinking. I won't be offended."

He looked at her sadly. "Oh, I don't think it would offend you to know how much I admire you and your father. You're so strong in your faith. My mother was that way, and—believe it or not—I used to read the Bible and pray with Ma. But then. . .I got mad at God. I guess I tried to believe He didn't exist; otherwise, He'd have heard me begging Him, night after night, to bring back my father."

Now, as he spoke of God, new hope filled her heart.

"Luke," she reached across to squeeze his hand, "you've had a very difficult time, and I don't have any answers. Sometimes things just happen, and we never understand why."

"You haven't had an easy time of it, either," he said, holding her hand, "but your heart hasn't turned hard the way mine has."

He looked at her tenderly. Suzanne saw his expression and she found herself hoping, desperately hoping, that he loved her. But would he ever admit it to himself? To her?

"Sometimes when I'm with you," he said, "I can believe that life is good, that maybe things do work out. But then . . . ," his voice trailed and he dropped her hand.

Suzanne held her breath. "Luke, listen to me. Life *is* good. You can be happy again. You could start a new life here."

He shook his head. "Not here. This town is a reminder that we lost him here. I can't stay."

She bit her lip, wondering how far to go with this conversation. She wanted to plead with him to come back with them to the ranch, to let her help him heal. But Luke was his own man, and he would make his own decisions when he was ready. In the meantime, all she could do was offer him the kindness he needed in his life. And her love. When he was ready to accept it.

Should she tell him that? Wasn't it fair for him to know?

"Luke, I have to say something to you. You know I say what I think and. . . ." She glanced at the church, drawing strength. "I want you to know that I love you."

Luke caught his breath. For a moment, he looked stunned by her words.

Suzanne flushed, looking away. She felt like a fool until Luke's hand cupped her chin, and ever so gently, he placed a kiss upon her lips.

When she opened her eyes, he was looking down at her with a tenderness that melted her heart.

"I love you too, Suzanne. You're all I could ever want in a woman but. . . ."

He pulled back from her, dropped his hand, and stared off in the distance.

"It's hard for me to get past today," he finally replied. "Please be patient with me. Maybe, when I can put the past behind me and figure out where I go from here..."

"Luke, I want you to keep looking for him."

He nodded. "Maybe I will. I don't know where that search will lead me, but somehow I don't think I can get on with my life until I find him. I promised Ma."

She nodded. "I know. You mustn't give up! You owe it to yourself—and you owe it to him."

eighteen

When Hank returned to the doctor's office the next morning for more tests, Suzanne decided to run an errand. She had spotted a library near the doctor's office, and now she was sauntering among the shelves, looking at books.

"May I help you, miss?" The librarian called helpfully.

"Yes. I'm looking for a book on flowers; specifically, the names of all kinds of flowers."

The librarian pursed her lips. "We have a new book in from a publishing house in New York." She reached up on a shelf and pulled down a thick tome. "It lists not only flowers but plants and shrubs. Would you like to check it out?"

"Yes, I would."

It was a shot in the dark, as Pa would say, but why not give it a try?

&

Suzanne sat at the kitchen table with Miss Martha, listening as she went on about the challenges of growing roses here in the high country. When finally she stopped to catch her breath, Suzanne cleared her throat and glanced down at the open page of the library book.

There were so many different kinds of flowers. How could they possibly find the one that matched the woman's name?

"Miss Martha," Suzanne began, "I want to ask you something. You said you never heard of a man named Luke Thomason. Can you think back, fourteen years ago, to a woman who lived here—" she broke off, realizing she had no idea what to ask. "Well, we don't even know her name, but Luke remembers it was like a flower."

Miss Martha looked bewildered. "A flower? My goodness, there's Rose or Iris or...." Her blue eyes went blank. "That's all the names I can think of." Then she smiled warmly. "You really want to help that young man, don't you?"

Suzanne nodded. "If I read off some flowers, will you listen to the names and see if you can think of anyone you ever knew or heard of by those names?"

Suzanne could see by Miss Martha's amused expression that she believed they were not going to accomplish anything.

"I'll try," she said tolerantly.

Suzanne started at the beginning of the alphabet. Once or twice, Miss Martha interrupted her, asking her to repeat the name. Then she shook her head.

"Jasmine and...."

"Wait!" Miss Martha threw up her little hand. "Jasmine, that's a flower that blooms in warm climates."

Suzanne glanced at her, trying to hide her exasperation. She hoped Miss Martha wouldn't get back on the subject of which flowers were suited to Colorado's climate and which ones were not.

"I don't know," Suzanne sighed. "I never heard of it."

"Wait a minute," Miss Martha jumped out of her chair and began to pace the floor. "Tillie," she snapped her fingers, and hurried toward the back door. "Tillie, my neighbor, owned a dress shop on Pikes Peak Avenue fourteen years ago. Every woman in town wanted a dress from Tillie's shop. Since then, Tillie got out of the business. When she stood on her feet for long periods of time—"

"Do you think," Suzanne interrupted her gently, "you've heard your friend mention the name Jasmine?"

Miss Martha stared into space, her face perplexed. "I don't know why, but I'm associating that name with Tillie. I'll run down to her house and see what she has to say."

"May I go with you?" Suzanne asked, trailing after her.

❧

Tillie Ledbetter rarely ventured from her cozy frame house that sat serenely behind a picket fence. The health problem Miss Martha had referred to was apparent to Suzanne at once, for the woman's feet were so swollen she had dispensed with shoes.

Tillie was a large woman whose excessive weight had contributed to the swelling of her knees and ankles, but she chose to blame the years she had spent standing on her feet in her fashion shop.

Miss Martha first posed the question of Luke Thomason—had Tillie ever known a man here by that name?

Tillie shook her head. "No, don't recall anyone by that name."

"What about the name Jasmine?" Miss Martha prodded.

Tillie turned her large head sideways, peering at Suzanne. "You're looking for this woman?" she inquired, frowning.

"Yes, I am. Have you ever heard the name?"

Tillie nodded her gray head slowly. "'Course I have. She was a good customer many years ago, but then. . . ."

Suzanne pounced on those words, kneeling beside the chair and looking up into the woman's face. "It's very important that I find this woman. Do you know if she's still here?"

A look of disapproval sat on Tillie's face before she replied. "The top drawer of the desk there. The big black book." She looked at Martha. "I still have a list of my customers."

Suzanne quickly retrieved the book and handed it to Tillie. As the woman's arthritic fingers fumbled with the pages, Suzanne had to fight an urge to grab the book and flip through it herself. She reminded herself the woman was doing her a great favor, that she must be patient.

An eternity seemed to pass as a Big Ben clock ticked relentlessly from the hallway and Miss Martha flitted about the parlor, examining the withered leaves of an African violet.

"Needs more water, Tillie," she scolded. "Last year when I was growing—"

"Here it is. Jasmine Rogers. I haven't seen her in years." She looked at Suzanne. "There's a pen and pad on the desk so you can write down the address." She frowned again. "That's a poor section of town now. Didn't used to be so bad."

Miss Martha flew back to their sides. "Suzanne is trying to help her friend Luke find his father. The man was with this woman—well, maybe not this one."

"No, I don't think Jasmine had a man. I heard she got her heart broken years ago, and never had anything to do with men after that. But I seem to remember something . . . ." The frown deepened, then she shook her head. "My memory isn't so good any more."

"I think your memory is excellent," Suzanne said, jotting down the address. "If this should be the woman we're looking for, I'll be eternally grateful."

Tillie studied Suzanne curiously. "I don't know who this young man is, but you must think a great deal of him."

"I do," Suzanne replied, folding the paper carefully and tucking it into her pocket. "I do. . . ."

❧

Hank seemed ill and out of sorts, Suzanne thought, as they left the livery. She had insisted on leaving a note there for Luke, in case he stopped by to check on the team. Her note explained what she had learned and gave the address of Jasmine Rogers. She'd left a duplicate at home with Miss Martha in case he stopped there.

Foolishly, she had neglected to find out where he was staying. Now she was worried sick that for some reason he might decide to leave town without a good-bye.

"Daughter, you're getting too involved," Hank snapped, upon hearing her plan.

"Pa, you know you're just as anxious as I am to help Luke."

He heaved a sigh. "Do you think finding his pa will help him? And what about you?"

Suzanne stared at him. "What do you mean?"

"He's already told us, once he settles the score with his pa, he'll be heading back for Kansas."

Suzanne bit her lip, trying not to think of that. "I know, but we have to risk losing him in order to help him."

Hank turned and stared at his daughter. "Suzanne, sometimes you amaze me." A smile softened his grim expression. "I'm proud of you. Maybe I don't tell you that often enough, but you know I am."

"I know, Pa," she replied.

She didn't like words like this which took her back to the last days she had spent with her mother. Her mother had spoken of pride and love and. . . .

Suzanne bit her lip. Just because her father seemed tired and out of sorts, and prone to compliment her, didn't mean he was going to die.

She stared bleakly at the streets, seeing nothing as she breathed a silent, desperate prayer.

❧

According to the man at the livery, Luke had just missed Suzanne and her father.

"She left a note for you in case you stopped by," the burly blacksmith said, lumbering into a tiny office to retrieve the note that had seemed so important to the pretty woman.

Puzzled, Luke took the note, already worrying that she was giving him bad news about her father. Quickly, he scanned the neat handwriting, then stared into space.

Jasmine! That was her name!

Luke checked the slip of paper again, confirming the address, as the clopping of horse's hooves broke the sullen stillness in this seedy part of town. He drew rein before the cabin at the end of the street. This was it.

The wedding band was nestled deep in his pocket. He was glad Suzanne had refused to sell it. The ring would prove his identity to the man who had abandoned him. He was going to feel like a fool, seeking out a father who had run out on him years ago.

He tried not to think about it, for he might lose his nerve. He'd simply tell him who he was, show him the ring, and admit he was here only because Ma had begged him to come. Even now, he half regretted making that promise to her. But he had, and he couldn't bring himself to back down. He'd never broken a promise to his mother when she was alive. And—he glanced idly at the clouds—he suspected she was still watching him.

He swung down from the horse and stared at the dilapidated cabin, sadly in need of paint. He glanced at the row of cabins he had passed. The others were no better.

A shutter hung crookedly against a window, covered with cheap cloth. There was no sign of life about the house. Did anyone live here, he wondered.

Well, he'd come this far, might as well knock on the door.

He tethered his horse to a sapling and crossed the small patch of yard where no grass dared grow, only weeds interspersed with pebbles and broken twigs from the lone tree at the corner. His boots resounded like a drum beat on the rickety porch. Beneath his weight, one board shifted, and he quickly sidestepped it. The other boards were loose, warped here and there. As he hurried to the door, something scrambled under the board porch, and he wondered how many rats infested the place.

The rough wooden door looked as though it had never held a coat of paint. He knocked carelessly, not expecting anyone to respond.

Faintly, he could hear footsteps moving slowly within. His heart beat faster. What was he going to do if the door opened and he was staring into his father's face?

The steps drew nearer, approaching the door. His eyes flew back over the surroundings. No, his father was not here; he and the woman probably had stayed only a short while until. . . .

The door cracked, then opened wider. He met a pair of dark eyes in a withered face. The woman did not speak; she merely stared at him. She was a pitiful looking woman. This couldn't possibly be the woman his father had left them for.

"Excuse me," he removed his hat. "I was looking for someone, but I think I've come to the wrong place."

"Who are you looking for?" The voice was faint and

labored, as though the woman had a breathing problem.

He felt more ridiculous by the minute. Still, he remembered the promise and knew he must begin his search here.

"I'm looking for a woman named Jasmine Rogers."

"She moved away." She was about to slam the door.

"Did you ever know a Luke Thomason?" he asked, thinking this was his last effort to find them.

She hesitated. Her dark eyes ran over him curiously. For a moment he thought she wasn't even going to respond. Then finally she opened her mouth to speak. He regretted coming. She was obviously too ill to be standing at the door.

"Sorry to have bothered you."

He turned to go, fitting his hat to his head again.

"Luke?" the woman called to him.

He whirled. "Yes, that was his name. Luke Thomason."

"I know. And you must be his son."

His knees were suddenly weak, as if he'd been rodeoing for the past twelve hours. Stunned, his eyes flew over her.

"I thought you were a bill collector," she sighed.

"You're Jasmine?" he asked incredulously.

"Yes. You'd better come in," she said, opening the door wider.

He stepped on the board porch, vaguely aware of the scurrying underneath. His eyes swept her, taking in every detail. She was a tall woman whose thin body was wrapped in a worn housecoat. Her feet were bare, her toes gnarled. Her skin was blue, as though she were cold, yet it was a warm spring day.

He said nothing as his mind groped with the words she had spoken. Now he tried to put meaning behind them.

"Come back to the kitchen," she said, closing the door behind him as he stepped into the front room, a cluttered living room with sagging furniture.

His eyes moved over the room, seeking a clue to the woman as he followed her into the tiny kitchen. This room was even more cluttered than the other one. Every available space on the counter was filled with canned goods, pots and pans, medicine bottles. Still, there was a pleasant aroma of something stewing in a pot on the old stove.

She motioned him to the tiny table in the center of the room. One chair was pulled back from the table. He spotted another chair against the wall and reached for it. There was no tablecloth, no flowers to grace the center as there had been in his mother's kitchen. A chipped enamel cup held something dark.

"I was having a cup of tea. I'll fix one for you."

He couldn't respond; his tongue had gone thick. This woman obviously was a link to his father, and suddenly he found himself willing to do almost anything to find him. This emotion surprised him, for he had built a wall around his heart, trying to protect it from ever feeling the awful ache he'd felt as a little boy losing the father he adored.

The woman moved slowly about her tiny kitchen, every movement an obvious effort. She dumped something into a cup, pulled a kettle from the burner, and poured steaming water into the cup. She reached for a spoon, frowning down into the liquid as she stirred. Then she handed him the cup.

He stared at her. "How did you know I was his son?"

She sighed and sank into the chair, staring at him. She had probably been attractive once upon a time, he decided. Not the gentle prettiness of his mother, a coarser kind of beauty, perhaps. Her hair, like her eyes, was dark, streaked with gray, slightly balding at the crown. Her features were bold, her lips tilted downward.

"Because you look just like him."

His heart was beating faster. "Where is he?" he asked, glancing toward the back door.

She looked down at her cup for a moment, then looked back at him. "He's dead," she replied.

Luke sank back in the chair. Naturally, he had considered the fact that his father might have died by now, but somehow he was unprepared to hear that announcement spoken in such a direct manner.

"How long ago did he die?" he asked. His voice sounded scratchy; his throat felt tight.

She lifted the cup and took a sip of her tea.

Luke stared at her wrinkled lips, wishing she would hurry and speak the words, tell him what she knew so he could leave.

"He died fourteen years ago."

Luke's mouth fell open as his mind slowly began to react, counting up the years.

"Fourteen years?" he repeated, trying to recall just how long it had been. He had just turned twelve when his father had saddled up and ridden off. He was twenty six now. "He died soon after he came here?" He spoke his thoughts aloud. "Why didn't you tell us in one of your letters?"

"I need to tell you the story," she said, her breath rasping. "The whole story." She took a deep, labored breath, releasing it slowly. "Maybe then I can die in peace."

Scarcely aware of what he was doing, he lifted the mug and took a sip of the tea. It was a strong heady substance, racing through him, jolting some of the shock from his brain.

"When your father rode into town, I was working at one of the saloons. That's right," she said, observing the look in his eyes. "I was the very opposite of your mother, I'm sure." Her voice had grown stronger as she tilted her head back, staring at something on the ceiling. She looked at him again, and a faint smile touched her pale lips.

"It was love at first sight for me, but not for him, of course." She sighed, tilting the cup again. She closed her eyes for a moment, and Luke thought she looked ancient, though she surely would not have been much older than his father. That would make her. . .mid-fifties.

"I made a play for him right away. He ignored me, and every other woman, but I kept talking to him. He had just come to town, looking for land to homestead. I could tell he didn't hang out in saloons. He seemed uncomfortable. Then, as he was leaving, we heard a commotion outside. I followed him out the door."

She paused for more tea.

"A man had taken a horse whip to a young boy out in front of the saloon. It was a pitiful sight. Don't know what the boy had done, but he didn't deserve to have a beating like that. Luke stepped in."

She stared into space, her eyes glazed as though seeing that horrible scene again. Then she shuddered. "The man pulled a gun and shot Luke. He fell face down on the street, and the man yelled for the boy to get into the wagon. They tore out of town. The sheriff came but did nothing. Said Luke had no business interfering with a man and his family."

When she hesitated, Luke finally found his voice.

"But he didn't die then, did he? He wrote to us. . . ."

"I took him to my place, had the doc with him, nursed him day and night. You see, he didn't know a soul in this town. He was shot in the abdomen, a bad shot. I fed him broth, bathed him, cared for him. The doc said he would never. . . ," she hesitated for a moment, then looked Luke in the eye, "be able to have more children, or live like a normal person again. He was messed up bad."

Luke dropped his head, feeling all the love for his father surfacing from a remote corner of his heart.

"Luke, I never loved a man like I loved your father. I just knew I could heal his broken heart, and I didn't care about the rest. Kansas seemed far away, and I didn't realize then how a person never stops loving someone. I thought the family he left behind would get over him. I told him he should write to you."

Luke remembered the letter—short, vague, telling them nothing, really. *Why hadn't Pa mentioned being shot? It would be just like him not to want to worry Ma.*

"My mother wrote back, but she never heard from him until—"

"Until I wrote her, saying he didn't love her anymore, that there was no point in writing to him. As for your mother's letters, I never gave them to him."

Luke glared at her, a slow rage building in him. He stood up abruptly, bumping the table and causing the tea to slosh in its cup.

"Luke, he died within three months. I had so little time with him, but—"

"You had no right," he snarled at her. "I thought the person I loved more than anyone had abandoned me. We nearly starved. And Ma believed—" he broke off, staring into space. What had she said on her deathbed?

"I don't know what happened to your father, but I never stopped loving him, and I believe he still loves me. A love like ours never dies. Please go and see him for me. . . ."

"Luke, you need to know this," Jasmine continued. Her voice had grown weak, ragged. "He called your mother's name when he was sickest, and he talked about you all the time. He said it was the reason he tried to save the boy outside the saloon—the boy was your age. He'd have given his life for you, Luke; and I think for a moment, that boy became you."

Luke swallowed hard, as the anger began to fade. He sank into the chair, staring at this woman, trying to see her through his father's eyes. She had cared for him, done her best to save his life. He supposed he should be grateful for that. Still, he couldn't forgive her for. . . .

Forgive. That word stuck in his brain. He could never seem to get away from it.

"I know what I did was wrong," she continued faintly "If you knew how I've been tormented by guilt all these years, you would know I have paid for my mistake. I know I should've written, but it became so painful—I couldn' face it. What I'd done, who I'd become. Guilt is a terrible thing, maybe stronger than love, if that's possible."

She came slowly to her feet and walked unsteadily to a corner cabinet. Opening the door, she reached to the very back. He watched her with tormented eyes, still too stunned to anticipate what she might say or do next.

"Maybe you'll believe I'm telling you the truth if I give you this."

She pulled out an ordinary looking jar, unscrewed the cap, and withdrew a small leather pouch. He stared at the pouch, his mind tumbling back to the day he had said good bye to his father. His father had placed the pouch in a secret pocket sewn inside his plaid woolen shirt.

Now, Luke stared at the pouch, the image of his father' strong hands etched in his memory from that day.

"Take it," she said, "it belongs to you and your mother."

Luke took the pouch and opened it. It was filled with

money. He looked up at her, puzzled and confused.

"I never took a dollar out of there," she said, gripping the edge of the table as she sank slowly into the chair. "It was bad enough that I had stolen another woman's husband. Somehow I couldn't bring myself to take the money too."

Luke didn't know what to say. He looked from the money to the woman. "I don't want it," he said at last, thrusting it across the table to her. His hand touched the tea, knocking it over. The brown liquid seeped across the table. He set the cup upright and looked around for a cloth to wipe up the mess. The woman didn't seem to notice.

"Don't be a fool," she snapped. Her dark eyes bored into his. "I've been trying to figure out how to get that money to you and your mother. I was determined to think of something, but I was running out of time. . . ."

She had turned deathly pale. Her breathing made heavy rasps in the still kitchen as she reached for her tea.

"What's wrong with you?" Luke asked, watching her tilt the cup again.

"A lung disease. I haven't much time left." With shaking hands, she set the cup down. It made a hollow clunk on the wooden table, accenting the silence that filled the room. Jasmine lifted bleak, desperate eyes to Luke's face. "I don't know what kind of miracle brought you here. But I'm glad you came."

Luke stared at her, somehow pitying her, wanting to offer comfort, yet unable to do so. This woman had brought them years of pain and heartache. He didn't hate her anymore, but he was not ready to be kind.

He knew she had read the emotion on his face because she cupped her chin in her hand and closed her eyes, as though defeated.

"Please, leave now," she said, reaching over to place the pouch in his hands again.

He opened his mouth, started to speak, then fell silent, unable to find words. His mind was like a flying jenny whirling around and around, while his heart pounded and his hand tightened on the pouch. The leather was soft, warm. He looked at it, feeling the last link with his mother and father.

Abruptly, he stood, tucking the pouch in his pants pocket. Again, he tried to say something to this woman, but he could not; so he turned and walked out of the house, closing the door softly behind him.

nineteen

Suzanne paced around the waiting room of the doctor's office. Three days had passed, and she had not seen or heard from Luke. Suzanne and Hank had driven past the ramshackle address Tillie had scrawled on the paper, but upon seeing Smoky tethered out front, they decided not to intrude on the private moment. *He must've ridden fast, to beat us to the house like that,* Suzanne mused to herself. Had he found his father? Or had he found someone at that address who had sent him to another town? Why hadn't he let her know what was going on?

Her father was responding well to the medicine, and for that, she was thankful beyond words. Still, she couldn't stop thinking of Luke. She was ready to swallow her pride and try to locate him if he hadn't left town already.

She thought back to the conversation she and her father had had while James, Miss Martha's nephew, had driven them to Dr. Crownover's office in his small buggy. James was a tall, gangly young man of nineteen who vaguely reminded her of Art Parkinson, though he had more class. He worked for Miss Martha as chauffeur, errand, and delivery boy.

"I've asked everyone I've come in contact with about a Luke Thomason," Hank had blurted the name that was uppermost in their minds, though neither had spoken. "Nobody knows him; he must have left here years ago."

"And now Luke's gone too," she had responded with uncharacteristic pessimism.

Hank had said nothing more. She knew he was disappointed, as well. How could Luke have left without telling them good-bye?

"Miss Waters."

The sound of Dr. Crownover's voice pulled her thoughts back to the waiting room of the doctor's office.

Her eyes flew to the doorway of his private office, where he now stood, wearing what she hoped was a pleased smile. "Could you step in here, please?"

"Of course."

He was going to give them his opinion on Pa's heart condition now. She wrung her hands tightly before her and followed him into the cozy room where her father sat in an armchair opposite the doctor's desk. She settled into the other armchair, giving her father a reassuring smile.

The little doctor came back around the desk and took a seat. He looked at them with keen hazel eyes that had taken on a pleasant sparkle, Suzanne noticed. He shuffled through the papers on his desk, reading something briefly, then looking back at them.

Why doesn't he hurry and say something? Suzanne thought wildly, wondering if she and her father could contain their suspense for another moment.

Dr. Crownover cleared his throat. "I'm pleased to report that Mr. Waters' heart rate is slowing down to a normal pattern since he's been on the medication. And all the other tests indicate good health." He smiled, looking from Suzanne to Hank. "I believe you can go back to the ranch now. Just check in with me every three months. Or sooner, if there are any problems."

"You mean we can go home now?" Hank yelled, as excited as a child. "I'm going to be all right?"

"As all right as a man of your temperament can be!"

"Thank God," Hank said, dropping his head for a second.

Suzanne jumped up to hug her father. "Oh, Pa, I'm so relieved. Now we can go back to teasing and arguing and living a normal life!" She laughed as tears of happiness filled her eyes. She turned to the doctor, wanting to give him a hug as well. She refrained from doing so, sensing that such a gesture would simply embarrass the shy little man.

"The fussing will be up to you two," he grinned. "I am going to require him to give up his pipe, and limit his coffee to one cup at breakfast."

Hank moaned, but Suzanne placed a hand on his shoulder. "Can he still work with his horses?"

Hank's eyes shot to Dr. Crownover.

The little man studied Hank for a moment then grinned. "I wouldn't think of denying him that pleasure. Just be reasonable about doing anything strenuous."

A grin spread over Hank's thin face. "Thanks, Doc."

Suzanne opened her purse and withdrew the money she had earned on the cattle drive.

"We can't thank you enough, Dr. Crownover. How much do we owe you?"

The doctor shook his hand. "If you don't mind, I'd prefer to use your father as a guinea pig, so to speak."

Hank's gray brows peaked. "Beg your pardon?"

Dr. Crownover chuckled. "Don't be offended. It's simply a medical term for asking a patient to try out a new drug. You aren't the first patient to use this drug, but you are the oldest. I'd like access to use your records in my teaching and writing, if you have no objection."

"No, Doc. Don't reckon I mind if someone else could be helped."

Suzanne looked from the doctor to her father, then back again.

"You mean we don't owe you anything?" She couldn't believe it.

"You'll have to buy your own medicine when those I gave you run out," he said. "And the medicine is a bit expensive."

"We can manage," Suzanne said. "Thank you." She threw her arms around the man heedless of his awkward stance.

❧

"You two are setting off on that long journey back all by yourselves?" Miss Martha asked incredulously.

"Suzanne and I will make it just fine," Hank replied. "Don't trouble yourself any. Now, if you can figure up our bill, we'll be on our way."

Miss Martha fidgeted with her apron strings and shook her head. "I owe Mattie a big favor, one I'd feared I'd never be able to repay. She never comes to town."

Suzanne had entered the large kitchen, where her father was drinking a glass of ice water rather than his usual coffee. Upon hearing the conversation, Suzanne walked over to Miss Martha's side.

"I don't understand. What does your owing Mattie a favor have to do with us?"

Miss Martha grinned. "Well, seeing as how you two are special friends of hers, I consider you guests in my home. I couldn't allow you to pay."

Suzanne looked from Miss Martha to her father.

"Oh, no, ma'am," Hank protested. "We can't intrude on your hospitality that way."

She shook her head. "Mattie and her dear husband spent a winter here once. She became the best friend I ever had in my life. I can't count the times she insisted on cooking the evening meal when I was worn out or feeling poorly. This is the least I can do for Mattie. But," she looked Pa over with mischievous blue eyes, "you can pay me back by showing kindness to her. She's pretty fond of you."

Hank shuffled awkwardly, tugging at the lapel of his coat.

"We're fond of Mattie too, aren't we, Suzanne?" He looked desperately at Suzanne, trying to conceal his embarrassment.

"Of course we are. Mattie has become a good friend too, Miss Martha. And I think Pa feels the same way."

"Well, if we can't pay you, we'd best get on our way," he said, hurrying from the kitchen.

Suzanne stared after him for a moment, then looked back at Miss Martha. "I hope you don't think he was abrupt," she said, a bit embarrassed.

Miss Martha shook her head and grinned at Suzanne. "No, I just think he and Mattie are kind of sweet on each other."

Suzanne bit her lip, trying to suppress a laugh. "Well, that's fine with me," she said, hugging Miss Martha. "Thanks for all you've done for us. When we come back in three months, it has to be understood we'll be paying guests. Otherwise. . . ."

"All right, it's understood. I'll look forward to your coming. Just drop me a note in advance if that's possible, so I can have your rooms ready."

❧

Suzanne stood in the immaculate bedroom, her eyes scanning every corner. The cherry four-poster bed and matching dresser and washstand had been a sweet taste of luxury, a reminder of the home she had left behind in Denver. Yet, she did not feel sad about returning to the ranch. With extra money the doctor and Miss Martha had refused to take they could now buy another horse or two, and make it through summer. She was looking forward to going home.

She was saddened by the fact that Luke hadn't stopped by before he'd left for. . .wherever he had gone. But perhaps there was a reason for that. She had foolishly blurted her love for him—and he had expressed love for her. But he had also told her, in so many words, that he was not ready to settle down.

What had he said? He had to straighten his life out first. He had asked her to be patient, but what did he expect? He knew they would be returning to the ranch soon.

Maybe he had thought it would be easier for both of them if he left without a good-bye.

She reached down to snap the lid on her trunk. She had to stop thinking about him, but even as she made that vow, an ache filled her heart, reaching to her throat. She hadn't allowed herself to cry over him. She'd been too busy being grateful about Pa. And it seemed wrong, somehow, for her to be crying when she should be so relieved, so happy that the medicine was working for Pa.

Still. . . .

The trunk blurred before her as the tears she had fought now slipped over her lashes and down her cheeks. *I can't help thinking of him. And I can't help loving him,* she thought miserably.

There, she had admitted it again. Maybe she'd feel better.

James knocked on her door. "Are you ready, Miss Waters?" he called politely.

"Yes, I'm ready," she said, glancing around the room to be sure she hadn't forgotten something. "Come on in."

He smiled shyly as he entered, and she thought about how kind he had been to them.

"I hope you have a good year at the college."

Miss Martha had confided that her nephew was attending the prestigious college here in Colorado Springs.

"Thank you," he smiled.

She'd never get to go to college, but someday she would like for her children—

She halted her train of thought. It appeared unlikely now that she would ever marry. The only man who'd ever appealed to her had ridden out of her life forever.

"I've put your father's satchel in the buggy."

Suzanne nodded. "All right. I'm ready."

"Don't forget your letter," he said, reaching for the trunk.

Suzanne stared at him. "What letter?"

"The letter on the hall table."

Suzanne rushed past him, her skirts flying about her ankles. As soon as she spotted the envelope and saw Luke's scrawl, her heart began to hammer. She tore into the envelope and removed the brief note bearing today's date. *Today?*

> *Dear Suzanne,*
> *I came by to see you this morning, but you and your father were still at the doctor's office. I'll be back around noon. I have some business to take care of, but when I'm finished I'd like to see you back to the ranch.*
> *Love,*
> *Luke*

Suzanne reread the note as relief, then happiness, flooded through her.

"Pa, wait!" she called, running out the front door.

✽

Luke swung down from Smoky and tied the reins to a sapling. He retraced his steps up the walk to the same cabin where only three days ago he had heard the most startling story of his entire life. He had spent these past days alone in the boardinghouse when he hadn't riding over the countryside, pondering his life and his future. He had purposely stayed away from Suzanne and Hank until he had sorted through his feelings. Now he had—and he knew exactly what he wanted to do.

He stepped on the porch, avoiding the buckling board, hearing again the scampering sound underneath. He knocked on the door, then removed his hat, waiting for the slow thudding steps to eventually reach the door. Finally the door creaked open.

"Miss Rogers?"

He had been so stunned by this woman and the story she had told that he had overlooked some important details—like where his father was buried. He had found the town cemetery, however, and the tombstone marked Luke Thomason. He had stood there for a long time, making his peace.

"Hello, Luke," she said weakly. "Would you like to come in?"

"I can't stay." The words he had planned to say now hung in his throat as he twirled his hat in his hands and glanced back down the row of cheap cabins. "I went to my father's grave," he said, looking at her again. "The caretaker at the cemetery told me you've seen to its upkeep all these years. I really appreciate that."

She tilted her head and looked at him curiously. Then she smiled faintly. "I'll be put to rest beside him. I hope you don't mind."

It occurred to him he hadn't told her his mother had died.

"No, I don't mind," he said quietly. He felt sure the souls of his father and mother had been reunited. The physical aspects of life didn't seem to matter that much anymore. "Is there anything I can do before I leave?"

"Yes."

He waited, wondering what she would ask.

"You can forgive me."

His lips twitched as he tried to smile. "I couldn't have done that when I left Kansas. Along the way, I met a beautiful, kind woman. She and her father have taught me a lesson in forgiveness. And I've been doing some soul searching myself these past days." He took a deep breath and his smile widened. "I forgive you," he said at last. "Try to find some peace now in the time you have left."

Tears streamed down the wrinkled cheeks, and for the first time the dark eyes held an expression of hope.

"Thank you, Luke. And I do hope that you and your young woman find the love that," she paused, then continued, "your parents had for each other."

He swallowed hard. "Thank you."

❧

At noon, he cantered Smoky up Tejon to Miss Martha's Boardinghouse. He spotted Hank, sitting in a rocking chair on the front porch. Luke sensed Hank's restlessness from the way the rocker was moving back and forth in swift, almost frantic, motions.

When Hank glanced toward Luke, spotting horse and rider, his face lit up. He bolted out of the rocking chair and hurried down the porch steps to greet him.

"The medicine worked," he called to Luke.

Luke swung down from his horse and shook Hank's hand.

"That's real good news, Mr. Waters. I had a feeling everything was going to turn out just fine for you."

Hank nodded. "And what about you? We were anxious to hear but we thought maybe you'd left town."

Luke looked into Hank's eyes and shook his head. "I'd never do that without coming to see you first." Luke squared his shoulders. "My father died fourteen years ago. It'll take a long time to tell the story, so we'll have plenty to talk about in the wagon." Luke took a deep breath and spoke the words he had thought about long and hard. "I'll be accompanying you home," he said.

Home, did he say? Hank grinned. "Be mighty glad to have you," he said. "And I'm anxious to hear that story."

Luke hesitated. "If you have no objection, I'll be staying on."

Hank's brawny hand fumbled absently with the breast pocket of his shirt. "Keep forgetting I've given up my pipe. Luke, that's the second dose of good news I've had. My old ticker may get out of rhythm again!" Hank stroked his chin thoughtfully. "Luke?"

Luke was looking toward the house, and Hank figured from the wistful expression on his face, he might be hankering to see Suzanne. Still, Hank wanted to speak his piece.

"Yes, sir?" Luke looked back at him.

"There's no strings attached at my ranch. I'd never let my daughter talk me out of keeping my word like that low-down Godfrey fellow did."

Luke grinned. "Mr. Waters, I never thought of you as an eavesdropper."

"Nobody said that conversation was confidential, as I recollect."

"Well, sir, back to the subject of the ranch. What I had

in mind was a partnership with you. I have some money now."

Hank looked surprised. "You don't say? Well, sure. That's something else we can jaw on in the wagon."

Luke grinned and glanced toward the house. "Where's your daughter?"

"She went out back with Miss Martha to see that flower garden one last time before we go."

"I'd like to talk with her," Luke said, shoving his hands in his pockets. He turned and walked around the side of the house, his head bent, his brow furrowed.

He spotted Suzanne in the rear of the yard, bending over a rose bush. The funny-looking little woman had gone trotting back to the house for something, and Luke quickened his steps, seizing the opportunity.

"Hello," he called.

She whirled, and the thoughtful expression on her face turned quickly to one of radiance.

"Luke, I'm so glad to see you." She came forward and wrapped her arms around him. "Are you okay?"

Surprised and pleased, he hugged her back.

"I'm okay. More than okay." He reached down, tilting her head back. Adoring gray eyes shone up into his face. "I have a lot to tell you, but the most important thing is what I need to ask you."

She looked puzzled. He reached into his pocket and removed the gold wedding band. "I'd like to give this back again. This time, I hope you'll agree to wear it—as my wife."

Suzanne gasped. Her eyes dropped to the ring, then returned to his face. She smiled, raising her hand so that he could slip the ring on her finger.

"We'll need a ceremony to make it official," he said,

looking nervous.

She smiled. "I think that can be arranged when we return to Morning Mountain."

His lips came down, brushing over hers gently. Then as her arms went around him again, he pulled her against his chest, kissing her as he had longed to do since the day he'd met her.

When they broke apart, breathless, Luke began to chuckle. "I think we'd better plan that wedding pretty soon. Suzanne, I have so much to tell you."

"I want to hear! You have no idea how anxious I've been, how I've watched the window, hoping you'd come back."

"I'm a better man now," he said, looking with pride at this woman who had agreed to be his wife. "I have something to offer you. . . ."

"You've always had something to offer me," she said, reaching up to caress his cheek. "You're all I could want in a man. There's just one thing," she said, trying to think how to broach the subject.

"Suzanne, I've made my peace with God," he said quietly.

She looked at him for a moment, saying nothing, adoring him with her eyes.

"Then there's nothing more to say," she said, linking her arm through his.

"Morning Mountain," Luke rolled the words over on his tongue. "That sounds like a great place to begin a new life."

He leaned down to kiss her cheek. "For all the mornings of our lives. . . ."

A Letter To Our Readers

Dear Reader:

In order that we might better contribute to your reading enjoyment, we would appreciate your taking a few minutes to respond to the following questions. When completed, please return to the following:

Rebecca Germany, Editor
Heartsong Presents
P.O. Box 719
Uhrichsville, Ohio 44683

1. Did you enjoy reading *Morning Mountain*?
   ❏ Very much. I would like to see more books
      by this author!
   ❏ Moderately
      I would have enjoyed it more if _____

   _____

2. Are you a member of **Heartsong Presents**? ❏Yes ❏No
   If no, where did you purchase this book? _____

   _____

3. What influenced your decision to purchase this
   book? (Check those that apply.)

   ❏ Cover   ❏ Back cover copy

   ❏ Title   ❏ Friends

   ❏ Publicity   ❏ Other_____

4. How would you rate, on a scale from 1 (poor) to 5
   (superior), **Heartsong Presents'** new cover design?_____

5. On a scale from 1 (poor) to 10 (superior), please rate the following elements.

___Heroine   ___Plot

___Hero   ___Inspirational theme

___Setting   ___Secondary characters

6. What settings would you like to see covered in **Heartsong Presents** books?_____

_____

_____

7. What are some inspirational themes you would like to see treated in future books?_____

_____

_____

8. Would you be interested in reading other **Heartsong Presents** titles?   ❑ Yes   ❑ No

9. Please check your age range:
   ❑ Under 18   ❑ 18-24   ❑ 25-34
   ❑ 35-45   ❑ 46-55   ❑ Over 55

10. How many hours per week do you read? _____

Name _____

Occupation _____

Address _____

City_____ State_____ Zip_____

Hearts♥ng

Any 12 *Heartsong Presents* titles for only $26.95 **

HISTORICAL ROMANCE IS CHEAPER BY THE DOZEN!

Buy any assortment of twelve *Heartsong Presents* titles and save 25% off of the already discounted price of $2.95 each!

**plus $1.00 shipping and handling per order and sales tax where applicable.

HEARTSONG PRESENTS TITLES AVAILABLE NOW:

_HP 1 TORCH FOR TRINITY, *Colleen L. Reece**
_HP 2 WILDFLOWER HARVEST, *Colleen L. Reece**
_HP 7 CANDLESHINE, *Colleen L. Reece*
_HP 8 DESERT ROSE, *Colleen L. Reece*
_HP 11 RIVER OF FIRE, *Jacquelyn Cook**
_HP 12 COTTONWOOD DREAMS, *Norene Morris**
_HP 15 WHISPERS ON THE WIND, *Maryn Langer*
_HP 16 SILENCE IN THE SAGE, *Colleen L. Reece*
_HP 19 A PLACE TO BELONG, *Janelle Jamison**
_HP 20 SHORES OF PROMISE, *Kate Blackwell**
_HP 23 GONE WEST, *Kathleen Karr*
_HP 24 WHISPERS IN THE WILDERNESS, *Colleen L. Reece*
_HP 27 BEYOND THE SEARCHING RIVER, *Jacquelyn Cook*
_HP 28 DAKOTA DAWN, *Lauraine Snelling*
_HP 31 DREAM SPINNER, *Sally Laity*
_HP 32 THE PROMISED LAND, *Kathleen Karr*
_HP 35 WHEN COMES THE DAWN, *Brenda Bancroft*
_HP 36 THE SURE PROMISE, *JoAnn A. Grote*
_HP 39 RAINBOW HARVEST, *Norene Morris*
_HP 40 PERFECT LOVE, *Janelle Jamison*
_HP 43 VEILED JOY, *Colleen L. Reece*
_HP 44 DAKOTA DREAM, *Lauraine Snelling*
_HP 47 TENDER JOURNEYS, *Janelle Jamison*
_HP 48 SHORES OF DELIVERANCE, *Kate Blackwell*
_HP 51 THE UNFOLDING HEART, *JoAnn A. Grote*
_HP 52 TAPESTRY OF TAMAR, *Colleen L. Reece*
_HP 55 TREASURE OF THE HEART, *JoAnn A. Grote*
_HP 56 A LIGHT IN THE WINDOW, *Janelle Jamison*
_HP 59 EYES OF THE HEART, *Maryn Langer*
_HP 60 MORE THAN CONQUERORS, *Kay Cornelius*
_HP 63 THE WILLING HEART, *Janelle Jamison*
_HP 64 CROWS'-NESTS AND MIRRORS, *Colleen L. Reece*
_HP 67 DAKOTA DUSK, *Lauraine Snelling*
_HP 68 RIVERS RUSHING TO THE SEA, *Jacquelyn Cook*
_HP 71 DESTINY'S ROAD, *Janelle Jamison*
_HP 72 SONG OF CAPTIVITY, *Linda Herring*
_HP 75 MUSIC IN THE MOUNTAINS, *Colleen L. Reece*
_HP 76 HEARTBREAK TRAIL, *VeraLee Wiggins*

*Temporarily out of stock.

(If ordering from this page, please remember to include it with the order form.)

·······Presents·······

Great Inspirational Romance at a Great Price!

Heartsong Presents books are inspirational romances in contemporary and historical settings, designed to give you an enjoyable, spirit-lifting reading experience. You can choose from 144 wonderfully written titles from some of today's best authors like Colleen L. Reece,

When ordering quantities less than twelve, above titles are $2.95 each.